LIFE ON EARTH

STORIES

BY SHEILA BALLANTYNE

THE LINDEN PRESS   SIMON AND SCHUSTER

NEW YORK   LONDON   TORONTO

SYDNEY   TOKYO

1988

Copyright © 1988 by Sheila Ballantyne
All rights reserved
including the right of reproduction
in whole or in part in any form.
Published by The Linden Press/Simon and Schuster
A Division of Simon & Schuster Inc.
Published by Simon & Schuster Inc.
Simon & Schuster Building
Rockefeller Center
1230 Avenue of the Americas
New York, NY 10020
THE LINDEN PRESS/Simon and Schuster and colophon is a registered trademark of Simon & Schuster Inc.

Designed by Liney Li
Manufactured in the United States of America
1   3   5   7   9   10   8   6   4   2
Library of Congress Cataloging-in-Publication Data
Ballantyne, Sheila.
Life on earth : stories / by Sheila Ballantyne.
p. cm.
Contents: Untitled—ink on paper—Perpetual care—Mourning Henry
—Flaubert in Miami Beach—Letter to John Lennon—Pelicans in flight—Key
Largo—You are here—Letters to the darkness—Life on earth.
I. Title.
PS3552.A464L5 1988   88-1098
813'.54—dc19   CIP
ISBN 0-671-60547-X

"Untitled—Ink on Paper" first appeared in *The New Yorker* in 1976. "Perpetual Care" first appeared in *American Review* in 1976 and was later reprinted in *Prize Stories 1977, The O. Henry Awards*. "Flaubert in Miami Beach" has been broadcast on "Tell Me a Story," San Francisco, a National Public Radio station.

For B. For C. For D. For H. For Z.

I wish to express my gratitude to the John Simon Guggenheim Memorial Foundation for a Fellowship that has carried me, in spirit, far beyond the boundaries of this book.

❧ UNTITLED ❧

INK ON PAPER

H E THINKS it's because of Grave 7. He thinks: *She's been crazy before; everything goes back to the past. He thinks* it's because of Grave 7, too, for the same reason, but from a different perspective. There are two hes just as there are (at last count) two mes: the one who is married to him, and the one who is a patient of *his*. The two of them think there's only one me, because they're both reductionists. I haven't let on, because it's something that has to be picked up intuitively; if you have to explain, it's already too late.

I have problems like the following with *him*: *He'll* ask me something like, "How do you feel?" and there will be a pause, and then I'll answer, "I feel like the second movement of the Marcello Oboe Concerto in C Minor." And then *he'll* say, "Don't be obscure," and then I'll respond, "It's not obscure; that's exactly how I feel." Then *he'll* either remain silent, or *he'll*

let on that *he's* unfamiliar with the Marcello Oboe Concerto in
C Minor and I will therefore have to be more specific. As in
Verbalize instead of Allude. Then I'll remain silent, because I
can't do that.

With him, on the other hand, problems like the following are
more common: I'll open my mouth, the way people do when
they're about to speak, and he'll say, "Take it up with *him*." So
between the two of them, there isn't any alternative but to go
back to Grave 7. Sometimes I take the Marcello with me, sometimes not. It helps to have accompaniment when you're looking
for something. I should explain: I go there, but I've never been
there. Grave 7 has no marker; I just found out, after twenty-
seven years. It was such a shock, I go there almost every night
now, trying to find out if it's really true. I have no intention of
taking Mr. Vernon's word for it. The word of a man who would
name himself after his own cemetery is just about as suspect as
anything can be. However, for the sake of justice, his word
should be included in the discussion; truth is arrived at by the
inclusion of as many different perspectives as possible. I'd be a
fool to pretend otherwise. I try hard to be fair.

Your mother's remains were interred in Grave 7, Lot 279,
Section I, Mt. Vernon Memorial Park, in 1947.

Those weren't his entire words; no one gets to tell his or her
entire story. There isn't enough space. But the marker business
is important, so—Mr. Vernon again:

I might also mention that there is no marker on your
mother's grave, and if funds are available, it would be
nice...

Shove it, Mr. Vernon. Nice. Nice. Go on back in your vault
and have yourself a little necrophilia. (Over easy; sunny-side

up—courtesy Sunnyside Casket Co.; well *done!*) What a life; you could drop dead from the choices.

"There she goes again," he says, throwing his hands in the air, twisting the cork off another half gallon of Almaden Chablis. That's all he gets now that I've stopped feeding him. I never missed a meal, three times a day for fourteen years, until I heard about Grave 7. There was something about Grave 7 that reminded me of something long forgotten; someone out there who was supposed to feed *me* but got sidetracked in that maze Mr. Vernon now refers to as Grave 7, Lot 279, Section I. I've just got to find HER, there are no two ways about it. Mr. Vernon didn't include a map with his letter, but I know instincively that if he had, it would stagger the imagination and be impossible to decipher. You know those things without being told.

"I'm trying to understand, but you'll have to be more specific," he says, shifting *his* position in the chair, eyeing the clock. "I can't do something like that in fifty minutes," I answer. "I was only ten when it happened." The response appears, on the surface, to indicate risk, a willingness to fight amnesia; but all along, all three of us know it (*him*, me, and me), it's just another opportunity for *him* to think to *himself*, or imply, Well, isn't there a parallel here: SHE stopped feeding you; you've stopped feeding him. That's what I meant earlier about reductionism. The shortest distance between two points is the line connecting *A* with *B*. It's an easy way out, especially when time is running short and *he's* only allowed a half hour for lunch. I haven't yet found just the right explanation—the one that would let *him* know *he's* missed the point—but I'm working on it. I've thrown out a few clues, such as: It's always been like this between us; I've always known, just never realized; or, He's never fed me, not real food. I've just realized that, too, and *that's* the main reason I've decided to stop feeding him. But I don't think *he* heard me. I know as well as the next person that "tomorrow's another day," and I'll get another crack at it. But it's common knowledge that it's the nights that give the most trouble; it's those spaces in between that wear you down and compromise your best intentions. Even the living get sidetracked from time to time.

They both have a point, of course. Grave 7 is certainly in there, you can't deny that. Just what amount of weight, unit of measurement, percentage of importance to ascribe to it, however, remains a mystery. *He's* doing his damnedest, I suppose, to decipher the mystery, in *his* way. And, for his part, he's really counting on *him* to discover that Grave 7, in fact, carries a lot of weight, because this would let him off the hook, clear everything up, and get me back in the kitchen where I belong. I'm the fly in the ointment. I've had it with the kitchen; just can't stand the heat. I'm spending the days now trying to get my bill out of committee—the one that would give wives a depletion allowance—and nights looking for Grave 7. The neighbors think I've abandoned my role; but looking through windows you miss certain nuances, such as sound, and therefore never acquire the whole picture. None of us has it, either, and we're on the inside, so to speak.

Looming just ahead is a sign; it says, "DON'T FORGET HIM." HE'S in the picture, too. Well, I should have known it without the sign. But when you're just beginning to realize things, vision isn't as clear as you would wish. That makes three hes now, two mes, and one HER. It's getting crowded. Yes, of course, HE'S in the picture; HE precipitated the whole thing, after a fashion. HIS death left me with the dilemma of how to dispose of the ashes. And that led me to write to Mr. Vernon, which led to the discovery of Grave 7. I knew it was there, otherwise I wouldn't have known where to write; I knew HE was pressed for funds at the time (1947), but I didn't know about the absent marker. Actually, it's legal to scatter in this state, but it isn't in Mr. Vernon's. It would be so much easier just to spread HIM over some cow pasture and forget the whole thing. I can give myself no logical reason for wanting to put THEM together again; THEY managed apart for twenty-seven years. Still, in matters where you don't get second chances, it pays to consider things carefully. Do I want THEM to mingle? Or do I want the concrete container for HIM? Since SHE was there first, does that mean HE would be interred in the missionary position?

The law permits placement of cremated remains in an occupied grave if the family so desires.

If I say, "No, Mr. Vernon, I do *not* think it would be nice to have a 'permanent double-inscription marker' for the two of THEM," would that make me a bad daughter? And even if it did, to whom would it matter now? I'm already a bad wife, though I'm still a good mother; I feed them three times a day, all they can eat, in addition to the snacks. But he's always standing around with his mouth open, too, and that's where Grave 7 tipped the scales. How thin can you spread yourself? I asked, once I knew. He's a grown man; he can feed himself. I'd even forgive him for not feeding me if he'd just get off my back.

Well, look. You've got all these pressures on you, all these bizarre decisions to make, it's no wonder . . . This is what *he* is thinking to *himself* now, but I set *him* straight right away. I move fast because, although the time is running out (as it's wont to do), it isn't up yet. I say, "It sometimes takes just these kinds of things to make a person realize what she's been missing, hasn't been getting, and needs. You can't demand it of the dead, even if you could find the marker, so is it unfair to expect it of the living—especially the one who is living with you?" No, I stand firm; my vision isn't completely clear yet, but I can see that far,

at least. He never did the feeding because he always assumed
—and I concurred, until just recently—that it was his role to
pay the bills. I was the one who was supposed to serve up all
the meals. I'm not having anymore of that, because the Marcello is unequivocal on the matter; it says: You lost it then, you
don't have it now, and you've just got to get it somehow if you
want to stay alive.

Even if I find Grave 7, what could I say to HER? You did
your best while you were around? I don't blame you for dying;
how could any reasonable person do a thing like that? "But you
were only ten," *he* is bound to say. "A child cannot be expected
to be reasonable." Well, never mind, you may be right, but I
can't remember. Getting back to the present, can I blame him
for not being able to give what SHE gave, which was good
while it lasted but in the end not enough? And can he hold me
accountable for not being able to give what *SHE*—Hold it,
hold it. Who?—Christ. O.K. Now that *SHE'S* here, you've got
to introduce *HER. SHE* is the one who fed him before I came
into the picture.

I keep wondering if the canvas is big enough to support all
these occupants. Recent astrophysical findings, referring to the
universe, suggest that space itself expands, carrying its galaxies
with it. Every time I start to address myself to the question of
whether such findings can be applied to human relationships,
he says things like, "Your mind is in outer space; it's destroying
this family." The first time it happened, I admired his clever-
ness—was awed, in fact, by the accuracy of it: to have known
just where my mind was without my having opened my mouth.
They're not often able to do that; in fact, it's usually the other
way around. Don't I know—after fourteen years of "What *do*
they want?" and "What's eating you?" It's only been recently
that I've told him, using words, not symbols, what I want. He
didn't get the message, so I've placed an ad for an interpreter
but haven't had any responses yet. The eating question was

more difficult, it always is. *"You're* what's eating me!" I said, but he had a quick answer to that. "You're insane, you bitch; take a look at me: I'm starving." As yet, I haven't found a way to argue with logic as unassailable as that. It's probably got something to do with all the other things on my mind, like Grave 7, Lot 279, and so forth. If I ever got really technical—such as pointing out that in addition to the me who is married to him and the me who is a patient of *his* there is also the me who is the mother of them, and the me (it was just recently rediscovered) who is the daughter of HIM and HER—it would blow everything apart. So I just keep quietly to myself (insofar as that's possible in this menagerie), prowling the cemetery at night like Anubis, the ancient Egyptian jackal god, searching for food, markers, insight, evidence, whatever is out there that would throw some light on things and maybe also sustain.

He doesn't have to worry about markers and things like that because his *HE* and *SHE* aren't in the ground; *THEY'RE* still in the Bronx, feeding on each other in a way so familiar *THEY* no longer notice. There isn't much of *THEM* left, but *THEY'RE* still hanging on, providing a buffer for him between birth and death. When you have a generation above you, it acts as a cushion between you and all that space; you don't have to concern yourself with questions of mortality and infinity. That's why it's impossible for him to understand my preoccupation; he sees it as withdrawal of love, and that increases his hunger. They say adversity makes you strong (except in those cases where it makes you go under). I refuse to take this rap. Yes, I know Grave 7 is standing out like a sore thumb, and it's only a matter of time before *he* starts going up there, too, prowling around, looking for evidence that will support *his* case. That's precisely why I insist that *SHE* be represented in the picture, and not over in the margin somewhere. *SHE* overfed him; not only did it disagree with him, it was the wrong formula. He still calls *HER* long distance once a month and never lets on.

When I tell *him* I want to divorce him, *his* lips move slightly and, reading them, I make out something that looks like "Let's find Grave 7 first." *He's* a pretty good salesman, I'm impressed with *his* line, but haven't decided yet whether or not to buy. *He* sells other things besides ears. One of *his* specialties—you pick up right away that it's *his* favorite—is suspension of judgment. It's a sound product, except in cases where you've been using it all your life and feel the need to switch to something new. If you apply something like that to yourself indefinitely, the effect can lead to permanent paralysis. The FDA hasn't required that fact to be listed on the label, but any reasonably intelligent consumer can figure it out alone. The major issue still waiting to be settled, in my mind, at any rate, is whether all this has more to do with *HER* or with Grave 7. My natural skepticism would lead me to question whether issues like that can ever be "settled"; but I'm willing to sample suspended judgment—until Grave 7 has been exhumed. That doesn't mean I'm all reason —not by a long shot. At least once a week I bring up the subject of divorce, saying, "If I have to be alone, then I'd rather be alone *alone*," or something to that effect. He always says that was Marilyn Monroe's line, she said it first, it is not original with me. He's always trying to distract me, weaken my resolve with put-downs like that. But it doesn't bother me; I haven't read Marilyn Monroe, so as far as I'm concerned it originated with me, regardless of who might have "said" it first. It's nitpicking like this that drives me to the brink. It makes no difference if a thousand women said it; surely every human being has the right to express identical or universal feelings without being charged with plagiarism or infringement of copyright.

I think I'm beginning to go under. The effort required to be fair to him, *him*, HIM, HER, and them—not to mention me and me—imposes the kind of strain that sometimes results in cheating. The last two nights out there in Section I were particularly bad; they had me reaching for the Librium, the effect of which cheats *him*, eases things temporarily for him and them, helps me and me in the short run but cheats both of us in the long run, and has no effect whatsoever on HER or HIM. HE'S on ice for the moment, the crematorium having agreed to hold HIM without charge for thirty days while I make up my mind. The time is running out, which increases the pressure. The Librium is inimical to searches and decision making alike, but it gets you over the rough spots and through the night. Just before I reached for the pills, I was walking through the cemetery as usual, with my divining rod, calling "Mother!," tripping over all those other markers in the dark, when I thought I heard a voice whisper, "Over here!" But since the stick wasn't pointing down at the time, how could I be sure?

He's doing all *he* can to help, but *he* can't feed me. *He* hands me computer printouts from time to time. They say things like I*N*S*I*G*H*T, K*N*O*W*L*E*D*G*E, or U*N*D*E*R*S*T*A*N*D*I*N*G. They're not to be sneezed at, and *he* hands them over gently. But they are meant to sustain a different part of you than you think needs sustaining at the time. It takes everything I have to refrain from reaching for *his* hand instead of the message. I'm getting very desperate; I think: *Where am I going to get it?* Not from *him*; it's against the rules. Not from him; he's either holding it back, or hasn't got it, or has drawn the line at doing it in graveyards. Not from them; they're too little — they have to be filled up by me; when it reaches the top and starts spilling over, then they can give some back, but not before. Not from HIM; no way has been discovered to make ashes say "I love you." And least of all from HER.

In the dead of night at Mt. Vernon Memorial Park, it is very still but not completely silent. Deep in the folds of that manicured rolling earth, if you are patient and really have your ear to the ground, you can hear a voice. "I would hold you if I could," it whispers, "but you can understand my position." I think I've found HER! I would recognize that voice anywhere, even after twenty-seven years. Where is it coming from? Over there? Or is it there? Without a marker, it's hard to be sure, but I think I'm getting warm. Wait. There it is again. "Have you come to give me my marker? I've waited so long. You're the only one left who can give me what I need." Or did SHE say, "HIM! You're bringing HIM back to me, at last!" No, I think it was, "You're going to put HIM in here with *me?* After I had to *die* to get HIM off my back? Listen! Please . . . Don't you understand? I can't go through that again. HE never fed me! Let me RIP." Is it HER voice? Or someone else's? It must be HERS, all the others have markers; and it's obvious, even in the dark, only someone without a marker would need to call out in order to be recognized. What should I do? SHE'S not making any sense at all. And there's no one to ask this time of night. Mr. Vernon, he's down in the vault slipping it to some fresh corpse; who'd trust his judgment anyway? And he's asleep, he gets irritated if you wake him for no good reason; the kindest thing he'd say is, "Take it up with *him*," but it's after office hours. They're asleep, too, but even if they weren't, they'd just say something like, "Put THEM together so THEY'LL be happy." What do children know about these things? Most of their sweetest thoughts are based on absolute ignorance. It's becoming harder and harder to deny that I'm here; I've found Grave 7, even without the marker. I'd consider it an achievement if I knew what to do next. What a place; you could drop dead from the choices.

PERPETUAL CARE

DECEMBER 18

In answer to your query of December 3, the law permits the placement of cremated remains in an occupied grave, if the family so desires. In our cemetery we require that the cremains be placed in a small concrete vault. It is sealed when the cremains are placed.

Part of our charge of $152.54 is $75 for a permit to place another body in an occupied grave.

The only marking on your mother's grave is a small cement locator. This was put on at our expense to identify the grave, and it has the initials of the deceased and the grave location. A double inscription marker in your choice of gray, mahogany, or pink granite, size 32″ × 20″, complete with installation in the cemetery and inscribed with both names and dates, would be $250 plus state sales tax of $13.25.

We are enclosing the interment order showing the breakdown of expense. This form should be completed and returned to us in toto.

Cordially,

V. O. Vernon, Vice President
Mt. Vernon Memorial Park
Seattle, Washington

FEBRUARY 20

We have not received a reply to our letter of December 18, regarding placement of the cremains of your father in the grave now occupied by your mother.

We will appreciate hearing from you as to your decision in this matter so that we may close our file.

Cordially,

V. O. Vernon, Vice President
Mt. Vernon Memorial Park
Seattle, Washington

FEBRUARY 22

Hang in there, V.O. My father's ashes (or, as you people call them, *cremains*) are still in the humidifier up in the Reno crematorium. Your letters have been so—how shall I describe them? cordially obscene?—that I've been forced to consider Reno as the place of final burial. Actually, it's not just your letters, V.O.; the additional factor hanging over my head is the delicate matter of the mutual *couchette*. In addition to the oedipal considerations, what if I were to change my mind years later? I couldn't just dig them up and interrupt a thing like that. It would offend the average person's sensibilities, to say nothing of theirs, if indeed (admittedly, we're still in the larval stage of research on this) they have sensibilities. I can guess your position on this already, so I won't pursue it.

What I have to do before I can respond to your letter of December 18 is go to Reno to investigate the burial possibilities there. I have already made one abortive trip for that purpose (a week ago today). If it hadn't been for "the worst blizzard in twenty years" (why do they always say that every time it snows?) I might have made it. However, as things turned out, I spun off the road in my MG, nearly totaling myself as well as the car. It was a traumatic experience. I am very fond of my MG. If it had turned out tragically, would you have considered interring me in your cemetery with my car? In the grave now occupied by my mother? And perhaps also my father? The thought of it raises a host of interesting possibilities. You don't mind, do you, if I take a few minutes to describe my feelings? Actually, I'm kind of lonely, my husband and children are no help at all—no fault of theirs, you understand—but the fact is, I have this decision to make alone, and it's not easy, as you can see by my failure to respond to your letter of December 18.

Where shall I start? It goes so far back (I can hear you sighing; I know you run a business, but with your prices, surely you can afford to take a few minutes to listen to my explanation of why I cannot as yet reply. Do you have an adequate supply of cigars handy? Watch the ashes on your pinstripe.) To get back, the principal reason why the decision of *where to inter* is difficult lies with my ambivalent feelings toward him. Her, she's pretty much a blur after twenty-seven years; but him, more freshly dead, you know, bits and pieces still linger, still adhere to the mind. He did a lot of rotten things in his life, not the least of which were done to her; but still and all, isn't it true? what they say about death being the great equalizer? For this reason, it's

going to take a little more time, and another trip to Reno
(there was no damage to the MG; just a huge mass of snow
impacted in the radiator, which froze solid and made the motor
heat up and scared the shit out of me, as I still had another
thirty miles to drive in the blizzard, and it was getting dark).
Funny, but lying there in the embankment, becoming gradually
obscured by falling snow, came pretty close to the way he
himself met his end. Now, some would see this as sheer coincidence; some (my analyst, for instance), symbolic reenactment.
How do *you* see it, V.O.? (What does the V.O. stand for?
Victor Osborne? Vernon Oscar?) If you can just sit back, I'll
attempt to be brief, although it goes against my nature. You
see, I'm doing this mainly because I didn't like your phrase
about wanting to close your file. It had an abrupt ring to it,
made me feel about to be closed out. Explaining things to you
this way buys me a little time, makes me feel still "active"—if
you know what I mean. File-wise.

They weren't what you'd call the ideal couple. (But then,
who is?) I have the strongest urge to say that both tried their
best, but—in addition to the fact that they're both dead and
can no longer be studied—there are as yet no scientific means
by which to define what "best," in fact, really is. Therefore, I
won't say it. Rather, he gambled and drank, and she cried; I'm
sure you know the syndrome. In addition (there are a lot of
additionals in this account; I wouldn't be offended in the least
if you wished to take a break for lunch at this point. Matters of
reconstruction are always delicate and difficult. As an em-
balmer, you'll understand).

On the way up (I'm referring to the first trip to Reno, the
one I made in an attempt to settle this issue once and for all.
You know what they say: if you don't bury the dead, they can
hang around and affect you in various undesirable ways), I was
stopped for speeding by the Highway Patrol. It was my first
ticket; I've been driving for twenty years and had a perfect

record. As you can imagine, I had a lot on my mind at the time; it's not the most pleasant way to spend a weekend, driving four hundred miles round trip just to check out a cemetery. I imagine you, sitting at your desk, thinking I'm some kind of creep because I live in Berkeley and talk about inner meanings, but don't be alarmed because if the Reno thing doesn't work out, I definitely have not written off your cemetery as a possible place for my father's *cremains*.

To get back: I was traveling fast, but not without reason. The road report had warned of blizzard conditions up ahead and I was two hours behind schedule. Imagine my surprise when I saw the red light in the rearview mirror! He appeared out of nowhere, like a bat out of hell (as the saying goes). I had been very careful, looking to the left, right, and rear, as usual. The only possibility could have been a row of dense shrubbery about ten miles south of Vacaville, California. When you're going 85 miles an hour it's hard to keep your eye on every shrub—you've got the car to manage, and the road, in addition to all those maniacs who drive the freeway. This is what raced through my mind at that moment: twenty years down the drain, a perfect record blown to hell. But then the strangest thing happened. I received a mental image: a rough gray slab, it had all the usual on it—Here Lies, name, date, RIP—but what really caught my inner eye was the inscription: A Perfect Driving Record. I was collapsed over the wheel by the time he reached the window. He thought I was crying, as usual, what else are they to think when they flag down a woman? He assumed a compassionate face.

But, as it turned out, it wasn't a façade. Would you believe it possible for a highway patrolman to be capable of empathy? Not only that, he was proud of me. He scratched his forehead, pushing back his hat. He said, "You're really something! You were leaving them all *way* behind. I've never seen anyone like you!" I accepted it as a compliment, as I'm sure some small, uncorrupted part of him intended it. That tiny repressed aspect of his self that was born to delinquency reached out to that slightly larger part of my self that was born to same at that moment.

No longer wishing that epitaph for myself, I was free of striving for that particular perfection and thus had that much more libidinal energy at my disposal. Hence my ability to refrain from crying, pleading, and so forth. I did have to answer honestly when he asked why I might have been going 85 miles an hour ("I'm on my way to Reno to bury my father"). I know what you're thinking, it's the same as crying, but it happened to be true. For once, I was grateful to the truth for coming to my aid. He spent ten minutes over the hood trying to arrive at a fair reduction. He settled for going 65 in a 55-mph zone. I thought it very fair. He was like the father I never had. He even cautioned me, not in an authoritarian way, but with what appeared to be real concern: "Please try to stay somewhere within a reasonable limit." It was touching, I was grateful. Compassionate limit-setting, just what I always needed and never got.

Do you have children, V.O.? Do you give them the attention they require? or are you down in the vaults most of the time? I won't bore you with the details of what happened after that: stuck on Donner Pass for three hours; iced windshield wipers; broken chains. After the spinout, it was clear I wasn't going to make it to Reno; I spent the night at a friend's cabin, skied a little the following day, and took Compazine. I'm all set to go again this coming weekend, the weather report looks good, and believe me, V.O., if this doesn't do it, I give up. They can keep his *cremains*, makes no difference to me any longer, this has been the longest funeral in history, five years; don't you think that's enough time to have something like this on your mind? You're wondering about the five years. It was in all the Reno papers, but you probably missed it in Seattle; I would have missed it in Berkeley if the authorities hadn't called. He disappeared in the mountains in 1968 and they didn't find his bones until last Halloween. No, I'm not putting you on, V.O. Some hunter found the skeleton on Halloween. They couldn't find him at the time it happened because a blizzard came up (worst in twenty years), and the Civil Air Patrol couldn't get its planes up, and the sheriff's posse couldn't see where it was going. Three months passed before I stopped seeing him in my sleep. Now you understand my reference to the car in the snowdrift. Actually, the idea to keep (him) his *cremains* in Reno came to me on a chair lift; it was moving slowly past a stand of pines when I suddenly received the phrase about "Where the tree falls, let it lie." Know that one? and I thought, why not? Please don't be offended, V.O., I know yours is a much classier cemetery. I've given this matter serious and prolonged consideration. That's why I'm paralyzed at the moment. I'm counting on this weekend's trip to break that up and resolve this thing once and for all.

In order to know exactly what to do, what would be the "right" thing (you still believe in absolutes?), I'd have to make another trip, a major one, the one to my past, which I'm unwilling to do at this time, as my analyst can verify. It's funny, though, how you find yourself places, having arrived there by avenues that were not on the map. For instance, speaking just now of cars and mass burials reminded me of when we were all together, I was five, and he drove an old Ford, he and she would sit up front and I would be in the back. So if I had died in the spinout, and you had been good enough to inter me and the MG along with him in the grave now occupied by her, it would have brought everything back full cycle. It may not be possible to go home again in exactly the same way as when you left, but there are symbolic reunions still within our reach, don't you think that's true, V.O.? The three of us together again, in the car, it would have been so quiet down there, not like it was when she used to scream at him back in 1942. He was a real terror on the road; I know what you're thinking, but it isn't true. I have worked diligently for over twenty years to be unlike him in every way possible.

Well, V.O., it's been a pleasure talking to you, but I must close now. I'll get back to you after my trip to Reno and let you know my decision. And listen, you are not to worry; *nothing* could persuade me to go 85 again in that speed trap. In the meantime, keep your frigging hands off my file; I am definitely not ready to be closed out.

Yours truly

MARCH 5

V.O.—Here I am again.

How are you? I'm sorry I let Monday go by without writing, but I needed the extra day to recover from the weekend. As a man in a sensitive position, you'll understand. And then again, as a man who deals with death on an everyday basis (do you work on Sundays, too?), maybe you won't. After getting the children off to school I just sat and stared out the window, it was all I could do. The tulips are up here in California; how is the weather treating you there in Seattle? Rain, as usual? I planted three colors this year; red, orange, and yellow, but for some reason they bloomed consecutively, instead of together. (The reds first, then they died; and just as they were fading, the oranges opened up, and so on.) It affected me in a strange way, as though I should have known it would happen like that, but didn't, and then was surprised.

To get back to the business at hand, I know you're anxious to hear how things went. A lot happened, but not in terms of straight linear action, so if you'd prefer to save this until later, take it home with you, where you can read at your leisure, please feel free.

Where should I start? The sunlight on the Truckee River at 11:30 in the morning? With just enough snow in its color to contrast with the green underneath? It held such promise, it began to feel like the most natural thing in the world to be laying a ghost to rest. There was none of the fear that usually attaches to these things. Entering Reno, I began searching for the cemetery straight off. I guess it's safe to confess I felt a mild pull in the direction of the casinos; I thought, Why not throw one in the slot, for him. He gambled away all of his, and most of other people's. It seemed only fitting to make a gesture of that kind now that I was there. But you know how it is, V: First things first.

The Masonic Memorial Gardens is on the top of a hill overlooking the city of Reno. The dirt road leading up there nearly ruined my exhaust system. To the west the mountains shone in the midday light. Cattle grazed the length of the Truckee River. In my purse was a letter containing the name of the man I was supposed to see. It was a strange feeling driving through the gates, one of getting closer and closer to something you had put off as long as possible. What a place: everything spread out, disconnected, with little roads leading in all directions, then coming to a dead end. There were two mausoleum-columbariums, two offices, a garage-incinerator, and a trailer. I didn't know where to begin, so I went into the first columbarium and asked the caretaker where I could find Roy Granger's office. He was kneeling with his dustcloth at the foot of the niches, the glass-enclosed ones containing the copper urns in the shape of books with the deceased's name as title: a dark, dwarfed little man. He saw my camera and smiled. He had two front teeth missing. He said, "You take good pictures?" I became aware of a strange sound and, turning, noticed the twelve-foot water fountain cascading at the far end of the hall. It had orange spotlights playing on it. There were also six or eight gigantic tanks of tropical fish. Do you have anything like that in your columbarium? Well, you haven't heard the half of it, V.O. There were carpets, ramps, and (are you ready?) Muzak. But that isn't what knocked me out, the columbarium in Oakland has that—organ-music Muzak. My first visit there I went crazy looking for the man playing the organ. It wasn't until I'd covered the entire place that I realized it was coming out of the ceiling. No, it wasn't that the *trend* is undoubtedly toward Muzak in mausoleums. It was that here, in this isolated, architect-designed death house on a windswept hill, dead center of the Far West, they were playing "You and the Night and the Music." I couldn't help myself, V.O., I started dancing. The caretaker was in the washroom filling the water vases, I wouldn't have done it with him around. I danced up the ramp, past the colored fountain, to the upper level. By this time the tune on the tape was "It Had to Be You." I couldn't help slowing down, I was on the verge of tears.

Why do they keep columbariums humidified? Everyone's sealed in the walls. Except for the humidity and those file cabinets, it was just like a hotel. They had very nice furniture, pale oyster velvet chairs placed in strategic little groupings, lots of plants, miles of red carpets. I was the only one there. I stared at the marble walls, glowing in the humid orange light. One niche had fresh flowers and a note, one of those little florist cards. The message was handwritten, it read: Frank, I miss you and am always with you Day and Night we will never part your Wife, Rose Giannini. I found the caretaker and asked for directions to Roy Granger's office just as "The Blue Tango" started snowing softly down from the ceiling.

Now don't have a fit, I imagine you people aren't immune to class prejudices, but you mustn't make snap judgments. If you've never been to Reno, it's hard to appreciate that in spite of innovations such as the mausoleum I've just described, basic values still hold sway there. Roy Granger's "office" was a little room in the garage, off to the side of the incinerator where they do the cremations. The trailer next door is his home. It was way over on the other side of the cemetery. As I learned later, the place I stopped first was the Catholic side, they've got more money, that's why the colored fountain and the Muzak. Over on the Masonic side things are very simple. The grass was unwatered. As I pulled up to the garage it came to me for the first time that my father was in there. It was one of those things that you knew was impossible but true nonetheless.

It was hard walking in, but I forged on; I'd come two hundred miles for this. Incinerator dust glowed on the concrete floor. The only sound was the wind in the grass outside. I didn't shut the door after me, call it superstition if you like. Mr. Granger must have heard the car because this very large man came into the building right away. I said, "I'm looking for Roy Granger," and he replied, "I'm guilty." That's what I meant earlier about the straightforward simplicity that obtains in Reno. I extended my hand and he removed his hat. He was wearing khaki work clothes. He was maybe sixty-five or seventy. Did you know they still refer to people in his position here as sextons? It said so on the death certificate, which I received later. It was reassuring, the term sexton; it took me back to the early seventeenth century, the graveyard scene in Hamlet, to be exact, know that one?

Well, V.O., I know you're a busy man, and I said I'd try to be brief. Funny, I had expected Mr. Granger would be someone like you—with the pinstripe and a plush office; I had tried beforehand to prepare myself for it, I even considered dressing properly, but in the end, its being Reno, common sense prevailed and I was relieved that I'd decided on my denims, because here was Roy Granger in his khakis. It made what followed much easier. It would be stretching things to say I was relaxed, but I was straightforward. I said, "I've come to inquire about arrangements for placement of my father's remains." I couldn't bring myself to say *cremains*. In this atmosphere it seemed contrived. I knew that Roy Granger would have given me a funny look, as though to say, "That's the way they talk in the front office."

"Have a seat," he said. His desk was basic government issue, circa 1945. "I have a letter here," I said, fumbling in my Berkeley oriental-rug bag for the letter, "which states two choices: 'Interment in the columbarium niche, $100' or, 'Interment in the Masonic Memorial Urn Garden, $175.' I'd appreciate seeing the two alternatives before I make my final decision." Roy Granger smiled. He lifted himself from his chair and fetched the "urn marker" ($150 plus tax). I've never seen anything more disgusting, I'm telling it to you straight, V.O. He said the cost of copper had skyrocketed, something I already knew, I read the papers. Just a lousy 8" × 12" plaque for the name, date, and one-line sentiment, with a copper bucket underneath to hold the *cremains*. It gets inserted in the ground in the urn garden. I asked to see the urn garden, as well as the columbarium, where the $100 niches were. He was very obliging. We went out into the spring sun for our tour.

The Masonic columbarium is very simple. It is not architect-designed. Its interior is basic marble, with folding chairs, bare floors, and aqua altar accessories. There is, needless to say, no Muzak. The $100 niches were at the ceiling; they resembled post-office boxes. I said, "Show me the urn garden." It would have been an act of pure hostility to put him in a p.o. box next to the ceiling. I'm not saying he might not have deserved it, just that I couldn't do it.

The urn garden: Imagine an Olympic-size swimming pool. Now imagine it filled, not with water, but with dry grass. (Excuse me, V.O. I have to refresh my drink before I can finish this account. I don't know what your personal attitudes are with regard to drinking, but speaking purely for myself, I've found—somewhat late in life—it helps.) Thanks for waiting. There were six or seven copper "urn markers" inserted in the dry grass in the urn garden. They looked so lost there, it's hard to describe, as though there were no other "natural" setting in which to place the beloved's *cremains*, so the survivors, out of desperation, settled on the urn garden. The rest was vacant. It took less than two minutes for me to decide that my father wasn't going in there. I thought of him, a loner all his life: He would say, sometime after placement, probably the middle of the night when everything was quiet, What the hell did she put me here for? Who are all these assholes next to me? What in the name of Jesus am I doing in an Olympic-size urn garden?

On the way back to the garage Roy Granger opened up. He told me his personal philosophy. I think he sensed my thoughts, and having satisfied his obligation toward impartiality and professionalism, felt free to speak. "You know, when you've been here as long as I have," he said, "you get philosophical." I prepared myself to endure his philosophy. It came as a surprise when his philosophy touched something very deep in me. He said, "I had a heart attack last year, my third, and my wife and I, we've got a will. It states, whichever one goes first, the other scatters. If both of us go together, the eldest child scatters. It's the only way." We continued walking. I listened. The wind stirred the dry grass. He was so tall, Roy was. He walked in a heavy, lilting way that was perfectly attuned to the natural surroundings. I had a brief flash that it was just like walking beside a father, but repressed it. He told me of a woman in Reno who had her husband cremated and then asked him to sculpt a box in the shape of dice and paint the little dots on it; then she put her husband's *cremains* in it and put it on her mantel. Roy is a very respectful person, he didn't derogate her, but he mentioned it as an example of individual inclinations bordering on the bizarre. Needless to say, he complied with her request. Another one he was asked to cremate in an $800 coffin. I forget if it was rosewood or walnut. I think the body was in it for about an hour and a half, however long it took for the ceremony. Now you have to understand Roy is a tolerant person, but also practical. His blood pressure rose some describing this. It was clear he considered it a waste. It was also clear he considered it an individual right to make such a request, and his individual responsibility to honor it. As we walked, I felt very warm toward Roy Granger. I wish you could have seen the mountains in the distance that day, V.O.

Back at the incinerator, Roy walked over to a shelf against the wall. I knew immediately what was in there, and what he was going to do. He opened the door and ran his fingers down the row of 8 × 8 × 8 aluminum cans. His hand stopped when he came to the can with my father's name on it. My heart jumped. Does that surprise you? Don't think just because you do these things every day that others can adapt just like that. I thought, *There he is—so small, reduced to that.* "Here it is," he said, lifting the can from the shelf. He shook it lightly. I was shocked to hear the sound of bones against the aluminum. Why do you people persist in referring to what's left as *cremains* or *ashes?* when all the time it's fragments of bone? At this point, I wanted to turn and run. My throat was very dry. Roy Granger started to remove the masking tape around the top of the aluminum box. "Please don't do that"—I heard myself saying—"I haven't been here as long as you have, I am not 'philosophical.'"

"Oh, it's just bones, they're all the same," he smiled. "Come over here, I'll show you someone I 'did' yesterday." He led me toward the incinerator. I had averted my eyes from it from the start. There was a trough leading from the main body of the incinerator. I forced myself to keep my eyes open. In the trough were bones. Hip bones. Shoulder bones. Sockets, joints, even a partial skull. "He was a large man," Roy said. I confess my shock. Expecting ashes, then seeing the dry, pocked surface of a partial skull. However, I looked. I looked a long time. If I could absorb this "large man"—yesterday's *cremains*—maybe I could look at my father, it was within the realm of possibility.

We returned to the office. I said, "I have to think things over. I'll be back in an hour." Roy said, "I'll be here until four-thirty." I got back in the MG and headed for town. I went into Harrah's Club. It was so hot in there, breathing was difficult. I tried to make my way to the bar but it was wall-to-wall people, as they say here in California. I stood outside the circle of people crowded around the bar. On my right was a man, some-where around sixty-five or seventy. He turned and put his arm around me and said, "You're so thin, I think we can squeeze you in here." I didn't recoil, not at all, in Reno things are very loose, basic, and simple. He had a sweet, defeated smile. Fi-nally I caught the bartender's eye. As I paid for the drink I realized that the man's arm was still around my waist. He was so lonely, there was nothing sexual about it; didn't you know, V.O., that in casinos sex is unheard of? it's all money and de-spair. So I lingered a few minutes, he was speaking of Bill Har-rah, the owner, how he was a "dear personal friend" of his. He sounded so much like my father, what else could I do but let him go on, about how people like us spend all our money here so that Bill Harrah can come walking into his casino with some wonderful thin girl on his arm. You don't have to be a certified psychologist to realize that he was thinking of me, for the space of that five minutes, as his wonderful thin girl, and dur-ing that time he was Bill Harrah and his grief lessened. I thanked him and wished him luck, told him not to give it all away to Bill; he laughed and I went to a phone booth and took a Librium and an aspirin, in that order, washing them down with the vodka and tonic. I stayed in the phone booth for a half hour, thinking.

The drinks there aren't strong, but it was stifling in the phone booth. I leaned against the wall, inviting visions. What came to me were mountains. When I was a child he was always going up to the mountains, staking imaginary claims; some were even in my name. When he was sent to jail for doing it with other people's money it caused me deep shame that it had been done in my name—my name stamped there on the complaint, and on the form in the recording office, on the mountain itself. (When you stake a claim, is there really a stake? Is it driven into actual ground? Does it bear a name the way a tombstone does?) It wasn't just the heat, some resolutions materialize with unexpected ease. Still, I wanted it to sink in before returning to Roy, so I made my way back through the crowds, the ringing bells, all that burning currency greased with sweat. The MG was parked in front of the Salvation Army, two blocks away. Tourists skimmed the sidewalks with their drinks in hand. I drove west along the Truckee River, wondering if I could do it.

I headed back to Masonic Memorial, up on the hill. To the west the mountains simmered in late afternoon light. Mount Rose was still covered with snow. Mount Rose dominates the Reno valley to the southwest. It is where, according to Roy Granger, many choose to "scatter." They still use that term, which, to most people's minds, applies to ashes. Don't fade out on me, V.O. You aren't going to like what I have to say, but I didn't like your letters either, so fair is fair. Roy Granger was in his office. I smiled. He knew what I was going to say. I said, "You're a lousy urn salesman, Mr. Granger. I've come to claim my father." He understood it as a compliment meant for him. He brought the box into the office and put it on the desk. I knew this part was going to be hard, but claim means the same as commitment. "Have a seat," he said, withdrawing the papers from the drawer. I accepted his pen and put my name on them. My father witnessed from the southwest corner of the desk. Roy was so cool, he didn't say anything asinine like, You made the right decision. He just smiled. V.O., I want to take this opportunity to thank you for your chilling cordiality, without which it is entirely possible that I would be, at this very moment, interring those *cremains* in the grave now occupied by my mother, in a small concrete vault, and watching the double inscription marker in my choice of pink granite being firmly fixed in place. I might be shaking your pink granite hand. Roy Granger put the papers in an envelope. I stared at the box. *Will he hand it to me?* was my next thought, which was immediately canceled by the knowledge that I was no longer a child; I had staked my claim. There is no other way to be rendered adult. I reached for the 8 × 8 × 8 aluminum box. I was unprepared for the weight. I thanked Roy Granger and walked to the car. I cradled the box/my father in my arm, it's the only way you can carry something that heavy. I put it/the bones/him in the trunk. The sound of the lid slamming shut had a jarring effect.

It was important to keep moving. I got behind the wheel and started back down the dirt road. I'm sure something in the exhaust system was ruined by one of those loose rocks. I wondered how I would explain having my father in the trunk if I were stopped for speeding. I was torn between ignoring the fact that he was in there, or playing with it. It was still daylight, so I played with it awhile, I said, Hi, Daddy. I hope you weren't jolted too much back there. Don't criticize my driving, I'm in the driver's seat now. This is your last ride. We've all got to stop giving the orders, and renounce our supremacy, eventually, that's what death is all about. I am not unaware of the things you did in your life, I never was. I am not claiming you in spite of them, any more than I could refuse to claim you because of them. I claim you because I am honoring something in myself, don't ask me what it is, this whole business is new to me. I am taking you somewhere special, I think you'll approve. I'm not sure I can go through with it, but I've amazed myself this far. Don't do anything unexpected. Help me.

Heading out of town, V.O., there was an old man sitting on a bench by the side of the Truckee River. His head was bent, he was reading a book. From the back he looked so much like... I thought there had been a mistake. The road up Mount Rose curved and twisted. The snow level was somewhere around 7,000 feet. At 8,000 feet, just below the summit, I parked the car. I lifted the box from the trunk and held it close. I told myself that was because I was afraid of dropping it, but there was a strange intimacy to it that was closer to the truth. I began walking through the snow, looking for a good spot. That was when I realized I had no shovel. I wasn't sure I could do this in the first place; now I panicked. What am I doing on the top of this fucking mountain with a box of bones and no shovel? I closed my eyes. It was freezing up there. Well, what did they do in the old days? I asked myself. Before shovels? I instinctively headed for a down-slope on the Reno side. When they found the skeleton, it had been lying under a tree. The reason I didn't want your concrete vault is because I believe organic matter should be returned to the earth, where it can do some good, however remote. In this case, it should be allowed to nourish something; they put bone meal on roses for that purpose, don't they? I looked around for a tree. They were all over the place, pine, fir; I began to go nuts: which tree? Don't obsess, I told myself, if you hang around up here looking for the perfect place, you'll end up being discovered on Halloween, too. I settled on a fir, partway down the slope, overlooking the valley. It had a large rock at its base. I thought: it will serve as a *natural* marker. As I bent down, an inscription went through my mind. It's really amazing, V.O., the things the unconscious serves up in moments of crisis. This one origi-

nated in the seventeenth century, too, Shakespeare again, from
Julius Caesar:

> The evil that men do lives after them;
> The good is oft interred with their bones.

I broke off a small branch from the tree and poked it in the
ground. The earth was soft and porous from all the melting
snow. There was just enough of it at the base of the tree for the
grave. I began to dig with the stick, it was very easy. Toward
the end, I scooped the rest out with my hands. I stared into the
dark space. *"I do not lie in't, and yet it is mine."* Now the really
impossible part: picking off the masking tape from around the
lid of the can. It had been sitting on the shelf since last November; it was stiff. I was glad to be a woman, that happens
sometimes, because my nails came in handy. I thought: will I
be able to look at the bones? I felt another surge of gratitude
for Roy Granger, the second or third that day. I pulled at the
lid. It wouldn't come off. It was just like what always occurs in
the movies, in the middle of a perfect crime: something totally
unexpected, and utterly trivial, happens at the last minute to
render worthless everything that's gone before. I tore off a fin-
gernail halfway to the quick before I realized the lid didn't lift
up, it slid sideways. My finger was bleeding all over the can.
This is the last drop of blood you get from me, I said to my father.
Well, don't be so rigid, V.O., you don't really believe there's
such a thing as unambivalence toward the dead, do you? Under
the lid was a paper towel. Jesus, all these obstacles, how much
longer do you think I can hold out with regard to viewing the
bones? You think you can prepare yourself for these things, but
if too much time elapses the whole thing can be shot in a
minute, the nervous system was designed to handle just so
much. Placed on top of the paper towel was a little card bearing my father's name and the information that this package

contained his cremated remains, and a statement to the effect
that he was F.D. in rural Gerlach, Washoe County, Nevada, on
10/31/73. I put the card in my pocket. There was blood all
over the snow. This is utterly ridiculous—I didn't bargain for
melodrama. The voice that reasons with me at times like this
said, This is an important moment, if you don't assume a reflec-
tive manner, the whole gesture will be without meaning. I
lifted the paper towel. *You* might be immune, V.O., but there
was nothing in my history that prepared me for this. There was
a brief flash of exhilaration, followed swiftly by a feeling of
profound shame, followed by the awesomeness of viewing
some aspect of a person which that person himself had never
viewed. I did not, I could not, dwell. I blamed it on the fact
that a cold wind was blowing, but that was not the whole
truth. I began to empty the contents of the can into the grave
with as much respect as was possible under the circumstances.
They tumbled out in slow motion, as in a dream. It seemed
that bones would continue flowing forever, the can would
never empty itself. At this writing, I remember only the shape
of one round end of bone, probably elbow, something that
once had fit into a socket. That was the last thing I saw as I
folded the earth over my father and pressed it down. My eyes
were tearing, I don't know if it was the wind or if it came from
within. I broke off a small piece of fir and laid it on top. I
scattered some snow over that, it fell through my fingers like
white petals from a flower. I imagine all people have automatic
gestures at times like this that bear a marked similarity the
world over. I stood there a short time, thinking that this was
the way people had buried their dead from the beginning of
time. It was overwhelming to have become an adult and also a
link with the history of humanity, all in one day. This letter is a
small token of my thanks to you, V.O., and to let you know it's
OK to close your file on me.

MOURNING HENRY

HENRY, HENRY. What am I doing here lying on your grave? It's almost three o'clock, the children will be coming home from school. Good mothers don't lie in graveyards while their children beat on the doors of an empty house. There are no explanations that would satisfy them, their father, the authorities, etc. Certainly not the camera: the way I'm lying here on my back, with the camera in full view, you know and I know it's a prop; but others don't. This way, if the maintenance workers come by, they don't call the police ("Say, there's this crazy woman comes here every day and lies all over the graves"). No, they see me adjusting my lens and go on trimming the rose bushes. If I lie face down, I feel your heart beating under mine. On my back, I get unusual pictures—for instance, this three o'clock light, the way it illuminates the grains in your stone. It becomes not just three dimensional, but four.

To mark the burial place
of the mortal remains of

John McKee,

of McKeesport, Pennsylvania,
who died in Oakland Nov. 20,
1860: aged 67 years,

and

Sarah Bryson,

his wife,

of Pittsburgh, Pennsylvania,
who died in Sonoma Valley,
December 20, 1860, aged 64 years.
This stone is here placed by
their adopted son
Henry

You didn't think I thought this was *your* grave, did you? No,
I knew all along. It's just that your presence is so palpable here.
The first time I saw this stone, I just sat down and cried. The
reason I take these liberties, the reason I feel close to you, I
buried a mother and father, too. I was a "natural" child, and my
own children are "natural" children; still, I think a case like
yours carries the greater weight: that one line, the simple statement, "their adopted son Henry," takes my breath away.

Going by the dates, you're dead, now, too. I don't know
where, certainly not here; I've done this cemetery top to bottom and it's two hundred acres. But you're definitely here. De-
votion is considered an old-fashioned word now, Henry. You
wouldn't believe these times.

For instance, you'd find it distasteful the way I blast in here
in my old car at nine each morning. At that hour, when the sun

is low, the gravestones rise erect and still with sharply angled light along their sides—the poor and rich alike. And the winding roads turn in so many directions, it's an excellent way to test drive, especially after a tune-up and alignment. I know it's incongruous, racing in a graveyard, but I like incongruity, you could even say it turns me on (that's how they talk now; it means "arouses"). On a few occasions it has even blown me away (i.e., "affected profoundly"). Sometimes I see everything as though on a screen: the small car taking the curves (never more than 50 mph, I do respect the dead, in spite of appearances). It's so bizarre, and thrilling in a strange way, because the car is the only thing that moves here: everything else is stationary, never moves, has never moved, will never move again.

I didn't bury mine at the same time or in the same place, the way you did. It must have been a shock, their both passing within a month; but in another sense, a bonus, a relief. You could face it all at once instead of spread out over many years —one stone, a package deal. If I had adopted a child, I could ask for no testament more fitting than yours. There is something about your stone that says more about you than it does about them. It must have been a lonely task, your being the only one. I imagine you kneeling here in 1860, this very spot. Henry, I see you: you have a kind face, tender lips.

I seem fated to drive in here each day, roar around, shed some tears, then go home to let the children in for snacks. I haven't mourned. If you were here, as opposed to having a presence here, I would ask how long it lasted, how you handled it, things of that nature. I feel lucky each time I drive out the gates and they haven't called the police. You think I haven't seen the way the maintenance men watch me take these curves? They're not really gravediggers in the classical sense, they call them maintenance workers now (just as garbage cans are known as ecology units). There is one, he has a beard and wears tight jeans. I think he has a hunch. Or maybe he just thinks it's erotic to see a woman lying supine on someone's grave; it's pretty boring work, trimming the grass and all. He has a strong body. I think he suspects something, but I'm grateful for one thing, he hasn't called the cops. When you're in the throes of something like this, you have to take it step by step. Both of mine are in separate, far-off places; I envy your geographic focus, the way you were able to honor them with a single gesture, as a unit. You just can't be in two places at once, you'd split apart.

Did you marry, Henry? Did you love? The two aren't always synonymous. Did you have children? There must have been times when, in spite of your love for them, you felt a sadness that your "natural" parents never knew them. That's probably the only pain they caused you; being a man; you can't imagine what some of my days are like. At meals, they say things like, "Do we always have to have this? I'm sick of always having this." Later, when their father comes home from a meeting, he'll say something like, "Don't you have anything for me to eat?" And I'll say, "I'm tired of cooking two meals each night." Then he'll go off to McDonald's, slamming the door. McDonald's is a good mother; keeps it cooking twenty-four hours.

Or I'll be sitting with a cup of coffee, thinking, *there must be more than this*, when I notice something a child has crayoned on the kitchen wall: a hieroglyph that will endure at least until they tear the place down to make room for a freeway: BOBBY IS A FUCER. They don't have spelling now, just free expression. She ran up to me the other day and said, "You have black spots on your lungs." They teach them that in school. I've made many sacrifices for them, and now they want to take my cigarettes, too.

My neighbor to the left is getting a divorce. Her husband wants to be free. My neighbor on the right is getting a divorce. His wife wants to be free. His wife and her husband are not being free together; they are being free with another wife and husband in different parts of town who also want to be free. My husband and I are still together, though. And my car gets twenty-five miles to the gallon. He'll say, "Your car gets twenty-five miles to the gallon; what are you always bitching about?"

Yesterday when she came home from school (I nearly totaled a gravestone getting back on time), the first thing she said— even before the door snapped shut behind her—was, "Melody's mother is getting a divorce because she wants to be free. When I grow up, will I be free?" I lit another cigarette and said, "I don't want to hear one more word about black spots on the lungs." Sometimes I'll take a tranquilizer, they have those now; it's like having a friend inside. It soothes like a mother, suffuses like a lover. There's never been a case of a defective pill.

They made a big deal out of Mother's Day this year: pictures, flowers, small ceramic ashtrays they made in school. The week before, when I was helping in their classroom, the assignment was: Write a Sentence About Your Mother. The children were hunched over little tables, composing and erasing. Stanley was really working up a sweat; Stanley's mother is schizophrenic, so the rumor goes. His pockets are filled with little candies; his teeth are rotten and he's only seven. He wears a hat the color of marsh grass; he never takes it off. No one has ever seen him smile.

Stanley can't finish the assignment. The teacher is getting impatient. She reads a few of the other children's sentences to stimulate the sluggards. ("My mother smells like perfume." "My mother is like an orange because oranges are nourishing." "My mother is good as sweet-potato pie.") Stanley sucks his candy and stares at the ceiling. I move in next to him; I say, "What is your mother like?" He says, "I don't know what she's like." I ask, "Do you live with her?" (You've got to ask that, they often don't.) He says, "Yeah." I ask, "Well, what kinds of things do you see her doing?" He says, "I don't see her." I say, "Not even at dinner?" He says, "I eat dinner in my room." I ask, "Why?" He says, "Because the TV's in there." I take another stab at it. "Where does your mother eat dinner?" He says, "In the kitchen." I ask, "Does your father eat there, too?" "No," he says. "He wouldn't marry her."

Stanley's eyes are like pale lakes in winter. I would love him if I could; the trouble is, they always transfer them, often mid-year; things are so mobile now, Henry. And there's the whole issue of reserves. I often feel I haven't enough for my own— that's the trouble with "natural" children; they can eat you alive if you're not careful. You can't blame them, you're as good as sweet-potato pie.

Will they think I'm nuts, lying here this way, stroking the ground? This dark marble, warmed by the sun, is smoother than skin; long grasses ripple like water in the wind. The elms above cry out in tones of low desire. The thing I like about this place, it never changes and it doesn't go away. It's the only thing they can't tear down to make a freeway. The gravestones seem to know it, the way they freely tilt and lean. Some have been here over a hundred years, like yours. They really made things to last back then. And they have a lot to say; it's a shame that no one comes to listen. Maybe that explains their contorted positions; it's the most agonizing thing in the world when no one listens. I respect how it feels to have to lean and wait, for what seems like centuries.

He's coming this way. I think he's caught on, there's no way out of this, I left the camera in the car. What's holding me here? I could just get up and walk away. He moves slowly; it would be pointless for him to hurry, there's all the time in the world. He steps with a lilt over uneven ground, his jeans cling tightly to his legs. Don't misunderstand me, Henry; I would give it all to stroke your hand, your tender lips. When he kneels down, I see his arms are dark from working in the sun.

He doesn't smile, but his touch is gentle. A strange wind rips like paper through the grass, *shh, shh,* it whispers, as he begins to move; everything else is still. His weight's a surprise, but the ground is softer than I would have thought; it accommodates.

FLAUBERT
❧ IN MIAMI BEACH ❧

HERE WE ARE on a train, going clickety-clack through Nevada; don't ask me why. Married, you find yourself going lots of places you didn't intend to go. The decision to make this trip went something like this:

"Miami *Beach?* In *August?*"

"They won't live forever. They have a right to see their grandchildren. It's been five years." And so on, into the night.

A streak of natural charity, coupled with a wish for my children to have grandparents, had me humming "Moon Over Miami" in no time. I even made a contribution of my own: "If we take the train, we can see America." Two days and nights, suspended in space and time: a chance to read *Madame Bovary* —an item, among millions, shelved for "the future." I'll get something out of this vacation yet.

I watch the sun set over western Nevada, recalling the phone call from the night before: "Say hi to Grandma, hurry up, it's costing a fortune. She's going to bake cookies with you when we get to Florida, aren't you, Mother? What? Any kind, it doesn't have to be fancy, it's doing things *with you* that they'll like. Grandma and Grandpa are going to be so happy to see you!" "They are? What do they look like?"

The train just stopped in Ogden, Utah. Four black teenagers climb on board; they're going to visit *their* grandma, in Chicago. They find their seats in the front of the car and turn their transistor up. I check my watch: it's three in the morning. It seems they're going to boogie all night. This is the first time I've thought, Go back to Africa. If they'd been white, would I have thought, Go back to Plymouth?

He sleeps beside me, his frame twisted inside the coach chair. He did this for me—that's what? twenty points? I get at least ten, maybe fifteen, for keeping the children quiet all day while he sealed himself in the club car ("Where's Daddy?" "Three cars down, getting drunk, leave him alone"). All marriages operate on a point system; after the ten-year mark you need a bookkeeper. It's impossible to say how many points I get just for going on this trip. He cheated, using blackmail, to get me here. That's worth at least fifty, my favor. He said, "The children need their mother." I said, "They're your parents, I don't have to go." He said, "The children will be devastated if you don't."

So now I'm staring out the window, watching Nebraska slip by. In addition to Flaubert, I now admit another long-awaited expectation: coming face-to-face with America. I feel I'm on the threshold of something so vast, so immeasurable, there are no words in my mind that would describe it. Watching the clusters of farmhouses flash by, I find myself dreaming of families and land. Nebraska evokes a keen nostalgia for something I've never experienced. I must be reading things in: it doesn't take much effort to imagine that home-baked bread and steaming apple pie. I stop, due to ideological conflict: I have no right longing for roles I'd be unwilling to adopt myself. Still, I imagine the seasons, the harvest, hard work, extended family, everyone with a special function, a sense of purpose, pulling together. A certain richness—who'd walk away from that?

Night. We're sitting together, our arms around each other in a rare display of unity; when you don't have to be cooking and giving orders, there's time for simple affection. The car is dark now, the children drift in chairs across the aisle. We're waiting till they fall asleep; then we'll go back to the club car and Flaubert. I'll have to read in the bathroom because the club car's noisy. This is the second night, and I've read two pages; but it's all right: there'll be time for Flaubert in Miami while the children are baking cookies with Grandma. We stroke each other absently as lights from distant farms roll by. The Big Dipper rocks back and forth to the motion of the train. The children slip into sleep, but we make no move to go. A blood-red quarter moon lifts over the horizon. I lean my head against the glass and stare at the stars and think about pair-bonding. I've done stranger things than this.

He lifts himself from his seat and feels his way down the darkened aisle. I take Flaubert in the bathroom and light a cigarette and get to page three. A woman from Cheyenne is leaning on the basin, describing the grandchildren she'll be seeing in Dubuque. I smile and listen, then return to the coach car to sleep. On the platform between the cars, I pause and lean out the open window. The wind is hot, although it's after midnight; it swirls in the vast night, snapping my hair in my face. As the train slices through cornfields I imagine myself in a farmhouse, saying, "The train's on schedule." Inhaling deeply, I think: *America*. I go back inside and curl across his empty seat and fall asleep to the strains of "Jungle Boogie."

In Chicago we rent a car and pull out onto the freeway; we'll be driving the rest of the way. Ahead of us lie Indiana, Ohio,

Kentucky, Tennessee, and Georgia. Somewhere in Indiana we stop to let the children smell the grass and pat a horse on the face. When we stop again for gas, I see a sulphur yellow butterfly flattened on the asphalt drive. I lift it up carefully and slide it between the pages of Flaubert.

At the Holiday Inn across the street, the clerk informs us that all the rooms are full. After three days of confinement the children are beginning to act up. My son limps around the lobby, his empty sleeve flapping at his side, crying, "My arm is gone, I have no arm!" I'd ignore this back in California, but it embarrasses me here. "Put your arm back!" I hiss, as the clerk stares from behind the desk.

They curl together in the back as we head back down the freeway. It's dark now, and suddenly a strange thing happens: the fields and thickets on either side are filling up with tiny lights. It takes a minute for the mind to register: fireflies, short-circuiting the night. I'm struck by waves of feeling that say, This is it! This is America! The real thing. Wasn't it there, in all the books? Fireflies on hot summer nights? They pulsate and flicker, mile after mile, as I struggle inside the car. I want to beat it off and lie in some field, but say nothing. We have to make Cincinnati tonight.

When we arrive at ten, everything is closed. The children are hungry; but even at the fast-food places they're putting chairs on the tables and sweeping up. We course through miles of lifeless streets looking for a motel and wondering if everyone here goes to bed before ten. Only the churches are lit, except for an occasional playfield that illuminates a night game. Baseball and church—this is America, I think, fighting the isolation.

The first motel is full and the manager says most others are, too. The Reds are in town for a game. But he locates an inn with the last room in town; it's eight miles away on the new freeway. We argue: I say we must eat now; he says no: the room comes first, then he'll go out for something. We locate the freeway and travel until it ends. It does not divert; it just stops. It isn't finished, we learn, back at the small roadside diner by the off-ramp. Their sign reads SOUL FOOD in red neon; but they're just closing, too. I could cry, but hold it back. He goes inside to ask the manager directions. A woman approaches the car. "Everyone gets lost here," she says, "even the people who live here." She gives me directions, which I write on the back cover of Flaubert. When he comes out, he recites the manager's directions. They are different from the woman's, and I point this out. By now, it's nearly 1 A.M. We head for the freeway again and take the last turnoff before the end. It leads onto a small road beside the tracks. He stops the car and throws up his hands. "You can't do that," I say. "Turn left."

"What are you talking about? How do you know?"

"She said left then right, then bear straight, slightly right, after the Sunoco sign."

"Are we going to die?" a child whispers in the back.

"No, this is an adventure," I say, on the verge of hysteria. I do not say, "It was *your* idea to push on to Cincinnati tonight. I think of fireflies and close my eyes. Eventually the tracks give way to tree-lined streets. Our inn is on the corner. We are welcomed in an impersonal way; behind us, the children drop exhausted to the simulated parquet floor.

We push on—through Kentucky, Tennessee, and Georgia. I begin to wonder, Where are we going, and why? We're in the middle of America, and we can't stop because somewhere grandparents eagerly wait. Georgia has a humid, underwater feel; young green crickets mix with yellow butterflies among the pines. It is here, in fact, in the motel with carpeting on the walls, that he tells me of his decision: "We're going to spend a day at Disney World before Miami; the children deserve some fun." Quickly, I weigh: Is it worth risking a fight in this motel at midnight in order to defend my vision of Disney World as a crime against humanity? "I want them to see America," I say hotly, "not Disney World." His eyes say, "Are you going to spoil my one vacation a year?" So this is what I did to my own children: I traded their souls for a fightless night, as the fur walls of the Six Flags Motel are my witness.

Outside Macon, Georgia, lies the Ocmulgee burial ground: Indian funeral mounds and relics of a culture that predated the ancient Egyptians. It is early morning; giant spotted moths vibrate among purple wildflowers. Below us, the riverbed resonates with sounds of primordial life. We are in the presence of something so ancient, yet at the same time so modest, it would produce chills, or tears, if there were time. I suppress an urge to lie on the mound until the stars come out to see how it felt to them then. We take a guided tour of the Earth Lodge mound instead. It is geometrically perfect; the entrance faces east, and during the equinox the sun comes in at a certain exact point. Here they worshipped fire as "a piece of the sun on earth" ten thousand years ago.

Would you prefer a cut, or gradual dissolve, to Treasure Island? With its banded pink flamingos and caged finches? ("Throughout the island, you'll meet a variety of exotic birds. For example, the Blue Pea Fowl, often white in color, can be recognized by their humanlike voices crying 'HELP!'") There are hundreds of tourists on the island with us, digging for the shells that were buried in the sugar-perfect sand by Disney World employees sometime during the night. Cameras click behind every bush. Everyone's oohing and aahing; they accept this replica as something authentic. The children's excitement angers me; I sit on the sand and watch teenagers blast by in rented power boats. There are thousands of people here in Disney World today and not one of them is cynical like me. He's probably right—I should see a doctor. Nobody reacts this way unless they have a serious inability to adjust.

I should do a flashback to Main Street, U.S.A. We had the first fight there, in the fake town square. "For Christ's sake, can't you show some enthusiasm for the children's sake?"

"HELP!"

"What?"

"Look! They've created a replica of America!"

"What's so terrible about that? Everyone's enjoying it."

"It's evoking things in me against my will! It isn't real! That's a crime, that's manipulation," and so on. Oh, I wanted it so badly, wanted to sit on the bench in the square with neighbors and talk about the weather, our children, the crops. I kept closing my eyes. What am I doing *here?* The real America is back *there*—I saw it from the freeway. A white horse pulls a wagon down Main Street, U.S.A. Walking behind it, a fifteen-year-old in Disney whites flicks manure into a little chrome dustpan. Grownups don't come to Disney World to cry, they come to be children again; shape up, I tell myself, you still have to make it through Pirates of the Caribbean.

We are sitting four abreast in little boats, descending underground on the flow of water-filled chutes. This is the illusion; actually, the boats are pulled along by pulleys and chains. I grit my teeth. We are moving slowly through a bayou; you can hear the water lapping at the side of the boat. We glide past little shacks on stilts; lights glimmer from their windows, it is night. It's all there: the blinking stars, the dripping trees; you can feel the Southern night. There is a heavy moon somewhere, about to come up. I begin to relax, letting the evocations wash over me: I've been here before; I have a strong conviction, even though it isn't true. Yes, this is the bayou, it is as it should be, I recognize it as an experience long forgotten and recaptured now with a gratitude bordering on ecstasy.

Then I notice it, off to the left. Then another, in the distance, flickering in some moss-covered tree; then three more, in rapid succession, to the right, over the water. Fireflies. Little electric fireflies, very clever; you can't see the wires no matter how hard you strain your eyes. I begin to flip out, he senses it right away. "Sit still in the boat," he whispers irritably, but it's too late, I'm off. I roll my eyes back in my head and let out a scream, but no one can hear it because we've left the bayou now and are heading into the "Pirates' Lair": they're aiming at us with cannons, they're exploding all over the place—POW! POW! POW!—so real, the children think they're being killed. I scream again, I'm really cooking now: "SCREW YOU, WALT!" (They can kill you for that here.) "Evoking longings by mechanics! Producing dreams by technology!" No one pays attention, there's too much gunfire, we're all under attack, but he manages another whisper: "I'm going to have you committed if you don't pull yourself together." Pull myself together? In this looney bin? Animated human forms leer at us from every side, draping hairy legs over bridges, singing prerecorded songs through missing teeth. I'm trapped in a cavern under the streets of Disney World, being assaulted by a hallucination that resembles reality. It seems like the most natural thing in the world to want to bring the person responsible to justice. I shake my fist in air that's thick with gunsmoke. The children are ducking imaginary bullets under the seat. I've just realized something shocking—this all began when I was young, unable to defend myself: in 1947, with "Song of the South." "Zip-A-Dee-Doo-Dah," Uncle Remus, down on the bayou, fireflies . . . This is the ultimate manipulation: to awaken in you as an adult experiences that were canned for you as a child. As we stagger out into the hurricane that has hit while we were underground, I imagine my children years from now, surrounded by the hum of insects, under a pulsating moon on a summer night somewhere in the future, saying, "It's not as good as Disney World."

• • •

We're here at last: North Miami Beach, that gilded tropical encampment where the elderly migrate to their last paradise; flock to the cardboard high-rise mausoleums overlooking the Winn-Dixie supermarket and polluted lagoons; come to die among the powerboats and pink flamingos. We enter the lobby of the motel, where whole families languish in beach hats and Bermuda shorts; they fill the couches and chairs. This is where I'm going to read Flaubert, I think, as we are shown to our room.

The next morning we move to another motel. "Short visit," said the clerk as we checked out. Was it the note on the dresser, suggesting that Maria Flores, our Cuban-exile maid, received substandard wages which the management hoped we would make up with a large gratuity? The note on the bathroom wall describing the penalties for taking towels to the beach? Or the sign in the children's nursery: DON'T TOUCH THE TOYS. PARENTS WILL BE CHARGED FOR BREAKAGE. I don't know. I tried and tried, but could think of no immediate way to save Maria Flores. We're down the road now, at the Surf and Sea, with cockroaches. The room's been fumigated and he refuses to move again. We have a Haitian-exile maid this time; her name is Cleante and she sprays insecticide each day. I say, "Please, no spray." She smiles so sweetly. "You no like?" I shake my head. She regards me quizzically; everyone else like.

Grandma's and Grandpa's grievances flow out in contrapuntal surges, filling the tiny two-room apartment. I sit stiffly on the sofa with the plastic cover and listen. The children sit in still confusion on the rug; he's the one whose arrival they've awaited, not theirs. It isn't hard to read the children's minds: they're thinking, *This is what grandparents look like. This is how they talk.*

"I don't care if she *is* your sister, it isn't going to work; it's her or me," she yells. Grandpa strokes his head, inhales another Winston. The veins in his wrists and temples throb. Grandma says, "I'm not getting any younger. I said to him, 'The tension with her in this apartment is killing me. She's got to go.' Now he blames me." She snaps a dishtowel in the air.

Driving back to the motel, a small voice whispers from the back, "Grandma and Grandpa don't like us; they're disappointed." My heart contracts, but I keep still; they're his parents, let him explain. He assures them it is not their fault; Grandma and Grandpa are having special troubles now.

This motel has a kitchenette. I pull two beers from the small refrigerator and say, "They're not interested in the children; it's you they want." I know what this means: He'll go to their place nights for pot roast; the children and I will stay here, eating Hebrew National salami sandwiches. I know what the next five days will be like, but say nothing; he's just come face to face with the loss of an important illusion. I hand him a beer and say, "I'll manage." What this means to him is that I am mature and understanding; I will not make him pay because his parents are preoccupied; I'll keep everything under control down here at the Surf and Sea, while he atones for having grown up and moved West. What it means to me is that I'll read Flaubert now and make him pay later.

Two days pass. He takes Grandpa to the racetrack so he can hear his side ("She just won't lay off! I'm torn between the two of them, can'tcha see?"); and in the evenings, he eats her food and hears her side ("So I said to him, 'Listen, Buster, ya gotta be kidding, all of us together in this two-room apartment? Ya gotta be nuts!"). While she's talking, Grandpa goes down to the apartment lobby to check the action. There is no place to sit; vandals stole the couch, lamps, and coffee table, and management did not, and has no plans to, replace them. There is a card game in progress, though, at a shaky card table in the corner: six old men in undershirts. The air-conditioner is broken.

I make Hebrew National salami sandwiches days, while the children watch the lightning out the window, and read Flaubert nights. *"'What better occupation, really, than to spend the evening at the fireside with a book, with the wind beating on the windows and the lamp burning bright?'" "'You're right,'" she said, fixing her large black eyes on him."* I get to the part where she grows bored with her husband and seeks a lover. The air in the room is stale with week-old insecticide; the Atlantic tumbles and breaks outside the window. I am here at the tip, the very edge of it, and I've missed the whole thing. My America has slipped through my fingers; all that's left is the flight home three days from now. I stack the dishes in the steamy kitchenette and listen to the sounds of traffic in the street below.

By the following day the children have come to blows. In a pause between showers, I drag them to a supermarket two blocks away and buy them crayons. As the checker rings up the sale, I throw in a copy of *The National Enquirer* as an afterthought. I have never done this before. Back at the motel, I put the children in the bedroom with their crayons and curl up on the couch. I don't know where to start (14 WAYS TO GET A GOOD NIGHT'S SLEEP, page 44. WHAT AMERICA NEEDS TODAY, by Billy Graham, page 5). I tear the wrapper off a Baby Ruth and lick my lips. *The National Enquirer* is full of miracles. *The National Enquirer* helps the people here keep going: these fragile hoards who have migrated from other ghettos, who sit all day in plastic chairs watching the ocean change mood. *"America needs a life-style that is based on a worthwhile purpose. I have listened to the old and young, to the affluent and the underprivileged. I have been repeatedly confronted by individuals seeking meaning and purpose in life."*

The bedroom door slams open. "He broke my yellow! It has no point!" I refrain from saying that nothing has a point, this is just the beginning. I switch on the color TV instead. "Be quiet and watch," I say, as it snaps and crackles (CHARGES WATCHING TV HAS MADE CHILDREN FORGET TO PLAY, page 46). Two more hours and it will be time to drag out the Hebrew National, then put them to bed. I stare at a photo of Carrol (Baby Doll) Baker and her new lover. (HOW TO AVOID FANTASIES THAT CAN CAUSE YOU UNHAPPINESS, page 14.)

Ten P.M. It is ninety degrees in this room and the children can't sleep. Through the open door, the beat from a Cuban band filters up from the beach below. They race out on the balcony in their nightclothes and I join them. A warm wind whips their thin garments, the black Atlantic rolls and crests in rhythm with the band. The children hop on small bare feet as the music rebounds off the whitewashed walls. I begin to move with the beat, in spite of myself. Down on the beach, couples are dancing; the white surf swirls around the silhouettes as their feet make circles on the sand. I am aching to join them, but by the time I get the children to sleep, the band will have moved on. He won't be home till late tonight. I gather their small hands in mine and we dance together on the narrow balcony until the song is over. There's nothing left to do but go back in and read Flaubert; isn't that why I came here? I know America's down the drain, but there's no reason the trip should be a total disaster—or maybe it's got no point, either, why should it be exempt? It was just another fantasy that can cause unhappiness.

LETTER
❧ TO JOHN LENNON ❦

WHEN YOU WERE KILLED, your son said, "Now he's a part of everything." It was hard to think of you that way at first; we're creatures of habit, wedded to visible form. But I've been known to address the elements myself—water, air, trees, and worse; so this didn't seem so strange. There's a reason for this letter, but let me give you some background first; if I said it was prompted by hearing your old song on the radio, what would that prove? Thousands of others heard it, too.

I'm writing from the kitchen in the back of the house, where I live under an assumed name. (Thousands also do, if they're women and married; things don't change that fast.) It's odd: the usual connotation of the term "assumed name" suggests things of an exciting and clandestine nature; but in this case, it's so ordinary. It reminds me of something a neighbor once said (she'd been complaining about her husband, their sex life to be exact); and when I asked her why she slept with him she answered, "Because he's there." Now, that phrase evokes Mount Everest, or at least a sense of adventure; isn't that what mountain climbers mean when they use it? I had a dream last week: I stabbed my husband and his mistress with an ice pick through the neck. He doesn't have a mistress, to my knowledge, and ice picks were before my time. Lately, there's been a surfeit of conflicting imagery—past and present, real and imagined—that I have trouble synthesizing into a coherent whole. At a party last Christmas I heard someone, referring to her breakdown, say, "I over-amped"; and at the time I felt the term was alien, and inapplicable to me. But lately, I wonder.

When the house was broken into last month, they took the children's rock and coin collections, in addition to the camera and TV, but that's not news these days. This morning's mail brought a form letter on police department stationery that began: Dear Victim. Then, after lunch, there was a phone call from the school; I recognized the teacher's voice immediately. She spoke slowly, in a low tone, and I knew right away that my son had done something unsocial, or hyperactive, again. She said, "There's been an accident. Your son was playing with Emily, and we don't know what happened because there were no witnesses, but Emily died." It stopped my breathing cold. After a long silence, she finally said, "I thought you knew Emily was the classroom rat."

I'm sitting at the kitchen table as I write, thinking my usual things (we're born; we live; we die). I'm off work today, waiting for the plumber to return and finish what he started Tuesday; someone has to be here to let him in. As I wait, I ponder things; what else is there to do? The children are still at school and the dishes are all done, although the beds are still unmade. I stopped making them back in 1971 after reading *Patriarchal Attitudes*.

I think, We're born, we cry, someone feeds us, we grow.

Things happen, many of them terrifying. We survive, thrive, then linger. It makes no difference in the end; the arrows all point in the same direction. (It crosses my mind: maybe you're not interested in inner news. Actually, you couldn't classify this as news; just a depressive front moving along the periphery of my consciousness the way the weatherman on Channel 7 describes a cold front as moving in along the California coast.) It just occurs to me: Perhaps it was a relief to finally be a part of everything. As though some final step were taken, however unwillingly, and a new dimension embraced. I just hang here on the edge, fearing it.

Take last Monday, when I fell apart in the Red Door Restaurant. The car was across the street for an oil and lube. There was no place to wait but the Red Door, Open 24 Hours. I sat at the counter and ordered eggs. They come with home fries and a slice of orange that no one ever eats. Toast is included, and there are three kinds of jelly. I settled in and looked around. You could describe the people this way: single individuals alone at the counter staring into space; and couples together in booths staring into space. The music system was loud, but not overpowering—just enough to interfere with thought, but not with feeling. It belted out tunes from an old track: "Brain Damage," "You're No Good." I tried to imagine the largo from the Bach Violin Concerto in G minor, but it didn't fit.

The waitresses all wore nameplates listing their "home" cities (Irene-Buffalo; Verna-Ogden; Sue-Pasadena). This fit. In all probability, everyone in the restaurant was from somewhere else, too. The thought crossed my mind that they were having a Miss Red Door contest—like the Miss America pageant—but I dismissed it right away, preferring to see the nameplates with hometowns as just a simple friendly gesture.

An inevitable by-product of sitting at counters and staring into space is that you start associating to things, and dreaming. And what surfaced that morning was a movie I'd seen on TV the night before. It was a Japanese film with subtitles, on the educational channel; its subject was the major traditional conflict in Japan, dating from before feudal times: the one between *giri* (obligation—both societal and familial) and *ninjo* (individual feeling, or passion). The narrator acknowledged that this conflict was not unique to Japanese culture, but was present among all people in all cultures. I think he also mentioned that it had been universal since the beginning of time (or at least since the dawn of human civilization).

There are just two characters, a man and a woman. He's married, with social and professional status to uphold; she's a courtesan. They have fallen in love. I tuned in in the middle, after they've declared their love and are preparing to accept its price (double suicide). There was a lot of hand wringing and high-pitched moaning over this as they walked together through the night. Their breath came out in little clouds. She said, as though it were a choice they hadn't considered, that she didn't want to die. She declared her love again, and he reaffirmed his love for her. You'd think that would make for complete accord, but this was a Japanese film. Its point was they were victims of cultural conditioning, unable to accept, or even perceive, other options. I have trouble with that issue, too; whenever it surfaces in plays or films, I focus intently, as though the doomed characters could read my thoughts: *Run away! Hide out in the woods and be happy.* I acknowledge I've never had the courage to hide out in the woods and be happy. Maybe we're more governed by *giri* than we want to believe, although everyone seems to be giving it the finger these days.

In the next-to-last scene they are walking slowly through a cemetery, and they pause among the graves to make love. Before you know it, she is lying on the ground with her head and shoulders on a tombstone, and he is there beside her, slowly kissing her neck, her breasts, her pale white belly, half-exposed beneath a black kimono. The camera moves up her body and stops: Her eyes blink slowly, twice. Her face is suffused with an eroticism so exquisite it melts the snow that has begun to fall. Just as he goes down on her, the censor inserts a black frame reading SCENE DELETED, but it doesn't distract for more than a second (though by morning the station had logged hundreds of complaints) because you find yourself thinking you'd defy death, too, for something that finely realized. Minutes later, the thought occurs to you that it would be hard to achieve such ecstasy in a graveyard in winter at night with snow falling, but you dismiss it as intrusive to the mood. After a beautiful, if improbable, night's sleep, they finally do what they know is right: he slashes her with his sword (chest, back, throat), then hangs himself from the branches of a tree. Imagine me at the counter, remembering this.

My tears were quickly disguised as a winter cold and suppressed. I had to force myself to achieve this, and this is how I did it: I told myself, No one ever sits at a restaurant counter crying. It is not culturally acceptable behavior. Sue-Pasadena, the hostess, would die of embarrassment; it's not her job to cope with that sort of thing. But the mind is an inventive organ—it searches for solutions right to the end. I tried to imagine a condition under which I could sit and cry until the car was ready, and what came to mind was that it would be possible if everyone else at the counter were crying too. I looked quickly down the line: six men—two business types, four blue collar; and two women—a housewife with horn-rimmed glasses, and a Hollywood matron with platinum hair. A few were attempting the morning paper, but the rest had adopted variations on the posture of staring into space. One idly chewed, another absently stirred. It seemed the most natural thing in the world to imagine them all in tears, and I slowly began to expect it. I watched them closely and waited. They were very unresponsive, but I had a few good moments: seeing us all in my mind, crying in mixed harmony, our sounds rising in a crescendo of relief, as Irene-Buffalo wrings her hands and Sue-Pasadena faints dead away behind the register.

Just before paying the check, I had a terrific idea for the future: You have two national teams—this could be soccer, baseball or football, it doesn't matter, except that football would be preferable because it's more brutal and direct—and you call them the Giris and the Ninjos. And once a year they would battle it out in a giant stadium while thousands scream their heads off. I see the Giri side of the stadium rather empty, but you can never tell. Actually, you'd probably have the same old configurations represented there: the impulse-ridden dreamers on one side, the tight-assed obsessives on the other. It would be a real tension reducer any way you looked at it, though, and when it was over, the winners could go hide out in the woods and be happy. The rest could go back to their jobs and families and continue holding up the structure of society, just as they've always done.

Speaking of woods reminds me of the field trip I took with my son's class last week. It was freezing, with frost all over the ground; the teacher dragged everyone out to a remote nature preserve to study "the habits of indigenous animals." What this meant, in actual fact, was that you were supposed to help the children locate all the varieties of shit out there and encourage them to use their minds to determine which came from which animal: ("See those droppings? What kind of animal do you think left those?"). This is known as a "Learning Experience." What you had instead was everyone stepping in it and lots of bad language and general cutting up. We were out there two and a half hours; it was one of the worst mornings of my life. I was impressed, though, with the variety: rabbits (little piles, pellet size); deer (larger clusters of same); scores of animals unknown (badger, beaver, fox, mole); and one award-winning pile in a stand of pines that deserved a place in the Museum of Modern Art, and was done by a bear.

It was hard trying to keep up an interest in something like that with twenty-five racially, sexually, and culturally mixed children going crazy and yelling insults at each other like "Get that fuckin' beaver shit off my coat!" I just stood there and contemplated leaping over the marsh and fading into the distance forever. It didn't surprise me, when a boy found a salamander hiding under a rock and yelled, "Kill it! Kill the mother!," to hear myself whisper, *Kill it with an ice pick; be sure you get it in the neck.* On the way back, the school bus passed a building where someone had sprayed: CIVILIZATION SUCKS.

In yesterday's paper I noticed they've drawn up a map of the city, with detailed plans for coping with the earthquake when it comes. Californians are good at planning for the earthquake, while simultaneously denying it will happen. Studying the map of our area, I noted that we live both on a creek (which will flood), and in the fire area (which will burn), in addition to being on the fault (which will open up). The article also mentioned that routes from the city would be sealed off by any and/or all of the above. I found myself unable to consider the assets and liabilities of moving, or the assets and liabilities involved in staying put, and consequently over-amped—which resulted in the paralysis of staying put.

I was pretty keyed up that night, but managed to make it convincingly through my son's bedtime talk. Actually, it was more of a lecture (No. 3—the sequel to No. 2, which compliments him on his fine mind). This one points out that while a sharp mind is an asset any parent would be proud of, it is worthless if it isn't accompanied by a kind heart. He lay there thoughtfully, his hair falling in his eyes, sucking the tip of his finger. At one point, he asked, "If I had been born retarded, would you be disappointed?" That was harder to answer than is immediately apparent; I had to consider the emotional subtext implicit in the question (would you still love me no matter how impaired?), and at the same time fight off images of how nice it

would be if we were all retarded; then we could be happy
(according to the theory that holds the smarter you are, the
more misery). I lay there beside him, imagining all of us sitting
there smiling, picking our noses, watching the sun come up
and go down. As soon as his breathing indicated sleep, I went
in the kitchen and flipped on the radio and that's when I heard
your old song. It threw me back into that time again, and you
were back then, too. You weren't a part of everything yet; you
were just getting it on, putting it out, hanging on the edge,
fearing it. You strained against the radio like some trapped
thing, beating your wings in the dark room, singing, "Whatever gets you through the night, it's all right, it's all right."
Later, I took a Valium, and sure enough, it got me through the
night.

I'm here at the kitchen table as I write this; there's a certain
stability, even comfort, in that. Maybe after the earthquake it
won't be so, but for now it's just as it's always been. And the
doors are double-locked in case someone tries to break in. For
the moment, everything is quiet; there is just your old song,
playing in my mind. You're on the second verse now, singing,
"Whatever gets you through your life, it's all right, it's all
right." It repeats and repeats, like a broken record, cut off before the end. I imagine you singing it forever, a modern lullaby.
It stops my over-amping cold.

PELICANS
⟩ IN FLIGHT ⟨

THIS IS CALIFORNIA, the western edge, as far as you can go.
The big quake, when it comes, will push the coastline back
a bit and split this landfill down to its false core, and all these
buildings with it. But for now, everything's the same. I'm sitting
on the beach, my Nikes by my side, my old jeans rolled up to
the knees. Some smartass kids came by about an hour ago —
cutting school and calling *me* a bum. "Hey, mister, you a *tran-
sient?*" Then they laughed. I laughed too, the way that they
pronounced it; they must be from the private school on Fourth
Street.

The old man is here, as always, standing with his shoes almost in the water, throwing crusts of bread to shorebirds.
Every time he swings his arm they jump as one and land a little
farther down the beach. Later, when the light begins to fade
and he moves on, they'll return — pecking the bloated pieces as

they bob with the tide. He reaches into his pocket's depths, broadcasting his crumbs with some deep faith—as though he'd been waiting all his life to feed something. He lifts his eyes as the pelicans fly over him in groups, unbent by their awkward weight and holding the air.

He's always here about this time. The bread is from his lunch, down at Bigger Better Burger on San Pablo. We see each other there, but rarely talk; I take my pictures, he throws his bread. He likes to listen to the conversations as he eats alone. You can tell he thinks of himself as not retired, but free. He has to cross the tracks to get to the shore and I've seen him squinting between the ties in search of flattened pennies, as he must have in his youth. He was nodding in agreement with Al, the demolition foreman, at the counter just this morning: Things *have* changed. Al was saying, "I watch my daughter with her kids. She'll say, 'Jason, would you mind not putting your feet on the table?' Can you beat that? When I grew up, no one talked to us like that! It was, 'Ya want your head knocked off?' But I'm not complaining. I turned out okay." The guy who wipes the counter nodded too. I remember thinking, If it were nighttime, this could be a bar. It's old-fashioned, the way things used to be. The old man likes the stories the regulars tell; you pick this up by his expression as he listens. "I heard on a talk show about these franchises they've got in the South: You go in, rent a gun, and blow things away—just for recreation—the way you'd, say, go bowling."

Someone new came in the other day, but no one minded— we're cool. He struck up a conversation at the counter. He said, "I hate those restaurants advertising 'ambience.' I was in one yesterday and it was so plain, I felt ripped off—as if they'd used false advertising to get me in. I asked the waiter—I was baiting him, but I was pissed—'Where's the ambience?' and he said, 'It's in the back.'"

The talk this morning was of poisons. It came up over coffee: someone stared into his cup and started talking about the water. He wasn't a nut; he'd seen an article on conditions down in Silicon Valley. It claimed that all those microchip million-aires are bathing in toxic water, contaminated by their own greed; solvents from their companies have leaked into the groundwater and penetrate their skin now as they shower. Peo-ple smirked, even as they recoiled; no one here has millions. Most of the regulars work, or worked before they were laid off, or got old. Except for Ernie's wife: she buys products. It's her guiding inspiration.

Then Evelyn said, "Bet you don't know what goes on in that warehouse over on the flats," and everyone looked up, their interest piqued. Conversation moves in themes here. Ike at the end knew; so did I. It's a place for freezing people when they die. She'd read about it in the paper. She's even seen their truck; she thinks it's used to transport bodies—what else could it be for, it's so big. It's white, with their slogan stenciled on the side in red: LIFE EXTENSION THROUGH CRYONIC SUSPENSION. People say, "Tsk!" and shake their heads. "They've got bodies in there, stored in cylinders of liquid nitrogen; it costs thousands of dollars a year. When they've found a cure for what they had, they'll unfreeze them and they'll live again."

"That money could feed the poor," someone inevitably re-marked. But mostly they were silent; it seemed a possibility so beyond what they could comprehend, what they had ever known, that when the talk resumed, it drifted quickly back in old directions.

"Whatever happened to strontium 90 in milk?"

"Or mercury in fish?"

"I remember strontium 90: you'd go to nurse your baby and suddenly remember that what was keeping him alive was radio-active. It was everywhere, even in you—you were the agent of it. Some days, the thought was enough to stop the milk."

"I was nearly poisoned by my car last week—fumes from the

exhaust were leaking through the floorboards. It's being fixed right now, over at Eddie's Muffler—he's the best. The proctologist of auto repair."

It could be a bar, the way they carry on. I was watching earlier when Rachel paused beside a booth to fish for a pill in her apron pocket. It was probably an upper, but you can never tell. Everyone's on something. For some, it's drink; others, Valium. Some do coke when they have money, or smoke grass when they don't. Rachel likes Ecstasy, when she can find it, but it's getting harder now. It seems strange to outlaw something with such a pretty name: a state that anyone would be grateful to be in. Some people I know have had to switch to lithium and stay there. I've stopped everything for now—as though to go back to a time when people were just themselves, and somehow managed that way.

Evelyn's bringing up the warehouse provoked a round of opinion on what happens after death. Nadine thought the soul moves on to another level, and what you do in this life determines if it's high or low. Rhonda agreed. But the young kid sitting by the door, he's too much. This was his theory: "You go to heaven and everything's just great. Just total happiness forever." He works over at the video-rental place. People were respectful, but you could see they didn't agree. Joe was more realistic ("Just live as best you can; after that, bye-bye"), but Patty—you can't say she wasn't predictable: "Your body decomposes and fertilizes the plants." Only Nick, who does the counter, had it right, if you ask me. He said, "On a deeper level, I'd like to think the soul lives on; but on an intellectual level, I think you're finished."

I'm down here how, watching him feed the birds. I just came from the warehouse; I wanted to see it for myself. It overlooks the bay, and if you didn't know what's in there, you'd think it was just another storage shed. They have a name: Trans Time, Inc. I just went in and asked around. It's for real. Out in the garage, where they store the chemicals, they have six capsules —two with bodies in them: a husband and wife in one; two heads and a disembodied brain in the other. I felt like running back to Bigger Better Burger to tell the folks; they won't believe it. But it can wait till morning; it's hard to sort your thoughts when you're given information like that, so I just walk the beach and think. The husband and wife have been in cryonic suspension for years. Storing a whole body until a cure for death is found costs from $80,000 to $100,000. There are living people on the waiting list; they've bought shares. They call it deanimation, by the way, not death. They've got heart-lung machines, respirators, and antifreeze; they prep them the minute they come in.

The old man is giving up on the birds; the sun is going down behind Alcatraz, a burning liquid red. I'm thinking of an article I read once on Walt Disney, how his life was devoted to searching for ways to make inanimate things move. He coined his own term for it, *audio-animatronics*. It's the guiding principle behind Disneyland. He had himself cryonically suspended when he died—which seems a contradiction, unless you think of him as visionary. I heard they did Roy Rogers' horse, Trigger, too. The two of them are probably down in Hollywood somewhere, chilled to the bone.

Another article comes to mind—a nutrition study at the university, using mice or rats—I think it was mice. It claimed that undernutrition fosters longevity; but I don't know. The undernourished mice lived longer than the ones who ate, but were they happy? Length isn't everything. What's the point of going on and on and always being hungry for something?

You have to imagine it: these people are serious. Deep inside that cinder-block building are the rockets with the bodies inside. And that solitary brain: bobbing in its liquid ice the way you'd picture pure intelligence pulsing in the farthest regions of space.

The old man was a professor; I found out accidentally, he doesn't talk much anymore. He was sitting on the stool next to mine and overheard when Rita poured my refill and asked if I'd ever gotten my graduate degree. It was so hard, that answer, because to say I'd dropped out explained nothing. In fact, it sounded like I *was* a bum—that's the way I'd hear it if it came from someone else. I cupped my hands around my mug and the longer I stared at the steam the more complicated the answer became. I owe the old man. "Wisdom isn't found in degrees, son," he said softly, and that was all. But the air, so thick I couldn't breathe before, now lifted and the color returned to the room. Rita laughed. "He should know," she said. It's true I walk the beach these days; in every life there's a period for that, or its equivalent—like time out. Waiting table buys me freedom for now. Berkeley's full of waiter Ph.D.'s; the conversation's first rate. I'm not on unemployment yet and don't intend to be. I observe the scene and develop my prints, and for the moment it's enough. It's my belief that nothing's wasted in this life.

I come down here to watch the pelicans in flight. Those birds! I shiver when I think of it: on the verge of extinction, the very edge. After DDT was banned, they slowly staged a comeback, contrary to every expectation. You see them differently after that. Ungainly things, more like beasts when on the ground. Prehistoric relics, weaving side to side, holding up those giant beaks. Yet when they fly, you're there too. I can't explain it any other way.

The wind just shifted, like a jolt; it nearly blew me over. I spread my hands against the sand for balance. I felt the earthquake, it's here at last. I hold my breath, but things seem calm. I must have had a vision, or a lapse—it wasn't a dream as we know them. Disney was there, lurching in his liquid nitrogen. I close my eyes, the after-image still before me, and it all begins again: his chamber shudders, bearing down. The walls of his tank begin to hiss, then finally crack. The rosy plastic corpse bursts through its boundaries and tumbles, buoyant, toward the sea. Behind us, the freeway buckles and the buildings go down like pins. Finally, there's the fire, all purity and light, and in its heat Walt Disney melts, and is reborn.

At times, it seems this pier stretches to infinity. I'm running down it now and breathing hard. The sun has given up—the Pacific just swallows it whole. The pelicans ride above me, lancing off the shades of wind, flying in place as though nailed to the sky, their beaks sharpened to dark points, waiting for conditions to change. My mouth opens on the cooling air and drinks it in. The way they move, they're not twelve, but one; not descendants, but the same pelican, throughout time.

❧ KEY LARGO ❧

NEAR MIDNIGHT, Lily Greenberg strains from the cave of her pillows and zaps the TV with a trembling thumb. Her breath comes out in little drafts between uneven lips. The screen explodes in stars of vacant light, then crackles as its wires begin to cool. She stares into its glassy, dark abyss as the remote control slips exhausted from her hand.

The bedroom fan circles slowly in the dark. Her eyes are closed now, her head tipped back; she can feel the way it interrupts the air, sending little humid shocks of change into her limp and dying perm. She'll have to get it done before the party. *Eighty years.* She repeats the words again—they make no sense. And yet her birthday is next week; her only child is flying out for it, from California, with his wife. They think they're going to use the opportunity to talk her into going to a nursing home; but she's not stupid. She'd told him on the phone. "Listen. David. You think I was born yesterday?" She's aware of the numbers, 80; but they're *out there*—they don't have to do with her. In her mind, she's twenty-three. Dancing at the Avalon after work on Friday nights.

The tears spring up—she senses them, without the light: a confirmation that the dancing years are gone. The stroke and broken hip—that's when everything began to change. She regards the two conditions as a single fate: The end of movement as she knew it. "Harry, Harry, Harry," she calls out in quiet cries that originate far back, beyond the heart itself.

"How will we get through this?" Ella wonders as the wheels touch down.

"One day at a time," David answers quickly. For two years, his mother has refused to talk about her situation. It's not as though he hasn't warned her of this day; the social worker, too—whom he hired to check on her when his father, Harry, died. Lily still can't understand: if Medicaid can pay for care in nursing homes, why can't it do the same for her right here, in her own apartment? Back when she could walk, her old two-room apartment was all she'd ever wanted; it was home. But after Harry's death, the old place seemed to haunt her.

"This sounds crazy," she told Ella on the phone last year, "but I know that Harry's here with me. I'll be watching the TV, then suddenly I'll sense something next to me. His spirit's here, I feel it. Does that sound crazy?"

"It's not crazy," Ella said. "I know what you mean."

"I told the social worker: 'I want one of those bicycles—the kind you exercise on. This leg just won't work. Okay, so I can't dance. I'll settle for eighty percent mobility. I can't just sit here doing nothing, day after day.'"

"She needs to get out of there," David said when she'd hung up. "Those crooks have raised the rent again, the building's going to hell." Later, when he thought that she was ready, he brought the subject up with Lily.

"Harry's spirit will go with you to the new apartment," Ella added.

"That's true," Lily had mused. The social worker helped her pack.

Now, two girls trade shifts attending her in the new two-room apartment. They're both grown women, but she calls them girls. "Miranda and Faye, they're wonderful girls." Two months from now, she'll have no money for their salaries. And he won't, either, David thinks. Both his parents worked so hard. Harry's pension, in the early years, was a thing of pride; in today's economy, a joke, a thing of shame. He runs his fingers through his hair and checks an impulse to rant against the government again; he knows what the humidity is out there, beyond the air-conditioned plane. The trick is to conserve energy. It will be a long week. He squints through the tiny window at the digital lights that spell out the Miami temperature. He draws a breath as he recalls the pearly fog that rushes nightly through the Golden Gate, surrounding the trees behind his yard. He's relieved that Ella's with him on this trip. There'll be the two of them to share the tasks that lie ahead. Maybe they'll get somewhere now; it's time Lily faced reality. It's time he faced it squarely, too. He tallies the appointments he has scheduled as the plane taxies slowly to a stop.

The visits to the nursing homes come first. The timing's late, and bad, and much of it is her own fault; still, he won't have her spend her last years in some place he couldn't bear to be himself. He'll investigate them all, and together they will choose the best. When her funds are finally gone, Medicaid will cover her. It's the least that they can do for making it impossible for her to stay in her own small place now that she requires full care. Two rooms can constitute a home; what do those idiots know about getting old? "This is my *home*," she cried fiercely into his receiver. "No one is going to take it from me." In frustration once, Ella had responded sharply, "Yes, they are, and there's nothing any of us can do." Lily had played dumb that time: she passed out on the phone; she fell immediately asleep. The social worker called him Monday. "Another move will be traumatic for her now. She must go through a process of giving up her things, and that takes time." Her first move, from New York, was not traumatic, he recalled. Fifteen years ago, she couldn't wait to go. "'A better life,'" she had quoted Sadie, the friend who'd moved the year before. Back then, she dreamed of palm trees; glassed-in shopping malls with aisles of gold.

David fiddles with the switches on the rental car as it leaves the freeway, turning east toward Collins Avenue. Ella turns the air-conditioner to MAX, the blower, HI. She stares out through the window as the air jets cool her hair. She turns her head as all the air-conditioned restaurants, bars, and lounges slip behind them, imagining their interiors: the small, low lights; and the two of them inside, giddy from exotic drinks and dancing to a small Brazilian band, stepping lightly out of this reality.

"I'd like to take you to Key Largo," he says suddenly. He took the children down there on vacation, years ago. She'd had to stay behind that year in order to complete some work. His father was alive then. They had all gone fishing; traveled out to coral reefs in sleek glass-bottom boats.

"It's a nice idea, but this trip's for Lily. We've got her birthday dinner to arrange; the nursing homes to see; the unveiling of your uncle's grave, the social worker's visit. We've got to get her settled." Her eyes drift out the window.

"I know all that. It would still be nice if the two of us could get away, even for half a day." They continue driving slowly down the street, past The Suez, Marco Polo, Blue Lagoon.

"I don't care where we stay, it's all the same to me." His voice sounds tired to her already, and it's only seven. The sun's still hot.

The next motel is modest, just three floors. A banner stretches out in front, above the office door: LOW LOW RATES. The man behind the desk is first to smile. "Sure, you can see the room," he says to Ella. He slides the key across the counter slowly, keeping three fingers lightly on, as though he had respect for it; he doesn't skip it hard, the way those acned boys do back at Tropic Towers. He has a salt-and-pepper mustache; his body's lean, his face is tanned behind the wireless wide bifocals. He's seen a thing or two, he has no ax to grind. "It's not an ocean-view," he says, his voice apologetic. "It's on the side."

The room is light, the drapes pulled back; beyond them lies a strip of ribboned sand: white, and stretching north. The marbled green Atlantic foams beside it. Ella bends to look inside the small refrigerator; its air is cold, its ice trays hard. She can see the two of them surviving here. If they can manage just one hour in that green sea, things are sure to come out right.

David pours a drink and dials his cousin Jerry's home in Boston. "Jerry's just been down here," he explains to Ella. "See that high-rise at the north end of the beach?" he said, pointing. "That's Jack and Poppy's place." Jerry's parents. David seems convinced that Jerry will have the latest word on Lily's mood —Jack and Poppy phone her every day, sometimes twice. "We're in a minefield, we need all the information we can get," he insists.

"Hi, Jerry. This is David. How are things with you?"

Ella drops two ice cubes in a plastic cup and pours the wine they bought across the street. She stands beside the window, looking north toward Jack and Poppy's building. Higher than the others, it hugs the shore, curving gently, like the inside of an arm. Behind her, David's voice is rising.

"I'm referring to what I said to you about what your mother allegedly said according to Lily."

His family's thick with secrets; it takes whole lifetimes to get the truth. She thinks how all five sisters on his mother's side were named for flowers: Lily, Violet, Iris, Rose and Poppy. She's seen the rusted photographs from when they all were young—their three dark brothers threaded in between, like trees. Vi and Iris were the first to go, then Rose; all that's left are Lil and Poppy now. Poppy is the eldest, ninety-one. Her eyes water, she forgets things; but she still gets around. Ella envied that large family when she and David married—as though its numbers were insurance against some unimagined future isolation. They had all lived near each other in the Bronx: some on the same block, or on adjacent floors—even in the same apartment. She'd had a mental picture of them: going in and out of buildings, establishing all those colonies within.

He dials Lily's number next. "Talk a little louder," Ella hears him say. He cups his hand across the phone. "She's in bed," he whispers. "The girl left the door unlocked for us."

"We'll be there after dinner. Right. Right. Ten at the latest." He remains sitting on the bed after he's replaced the receiver.

"We'll have to let her know the way things are," he says. "But we'll have to give it to her gradually, so she can absorb it."

In the restaurant bathrooms, the doors say GUYS, and DOLLS. Ella stands before the mirrored row of sinks, her feet spread and firmly planted as though she were still flying on the plane. She runs the COLD tap hard and brings her face down into her cupped hands. In the street, the air at ten o'clock is hot—like noon. As they cruise toward Lily's she opens all the cold air vents as far as they will go. David slows the car in front of Bristol Towers. The building is new; the mall across the street just has a K Mart and Winn-Dixie, but there is room for new expansion. They pause by Lily's door, then he knocks lightly and swings it open. Ella follows down the hallway to the bedroom; as she passes by her children's photographs in little frames on top of the TV, she jumps.

The king-size bed spreads out before them, nearly wall-to-wall. Lily nestles in the pillows on one side; the other side is smooth and undisturbed. She stretches thin arms out to them and they embrace. Her face falls on one side, from the stroke.

"Can I get you something to drink?" Ella asks.

"An ice cream soda." She articulates it slowly. "The seltzer's in the fridge—the big bottle. The cherry syrup, it's on the door. The ice cream's in the freezer. Don't forget the straw. They're in the cupboard, to the left."

Ella assembles things in Lily's kitchenette. She can hear their conversation in the other room: the children's summer jobs; Lily's recent visit to the doctor. She's glad for the distraction, she knows what lies ahead. If she can just create the perfect ice cream soda, everything will be all right. She'd expected the apartment to be tacky, but sees it has its own peculiar taste. She could imagine herself, years from now, finding comfort here. She can imagine terror at the thought of losing it.

Past midnight now, they sit side by side on dining chairs pulled next to Lily's bed. Ella tips back silently and waits; the air is sticking to her skin. "I turned the air-conditioner off to save money," Lily had announced when they'd arrived. She was being "good," thought Ella. So they wouldn't put her in a home. She hears David's voice as though from far away.

"This can't go on," he says. "There's no more money." Lily's eyes slip around the room, then settle on her folded hands— the hands that drop things now.

"You can't afford to stay here; and we can't afford the cost of full-time private care. The government will only pay that if you're in a nursing home. It's not fair, but there it is."

Her eyes squeeze shut as she absorbs his words as blows.

Her hands lie stiffly in her lap like statues' hands. Ella starts to cry. David reaches out and strokes her arm. "I'm sorry," he says quickly. He's not sure whom he's addressing.

Ella moves onto the bed and embraces Lily. "It's late," she says into the pillow. "We'll talk again tomorrow. We'll do everything we can."

"My bureau."

"What did she say?" David looks up, puzzled.

"She's talking about her furniture."

"I'm talking about my *bureau*. Can you two use it in your house in California? I wouldn't want to sell a piece like that. Harry picked it out with me."

"Let's talk about all of that tomorrow. You get some sleep," he says.

"Those movers wrecked my cabinet. They quoted me $275, then sent a bill for $450. They said it took them seven hours —does this look like seven hours to move these few pieces?" David's eyes are closing; he has heard this account, in all its versions, for a year now, by phone. Ella heard it twice, from him. Still, she nods, her eyes on Lily, as though the news were new.

"They were in the Yellow Pages: 'Nice Jewish Boy.' That's their company, it's right there on the boxes."

"She thought she could trust them with a name like that." David choked when he'd first heard. "Can you imagine? Taking advantage of old people that way?" He'd been close to tears. "What's this fucking society coming to?"

"They broke the legs off both my chairs. The social worker, she says she'll go to court for me. But I have to get an estimate."

"We'll talk about it in the morning. We have the whole week to go over things."

"Channel 4 had a special on what those people did. It was on the eleven o'clock news."

"Lily, let me turn the air-conditioner on before we leave."

"No, Ella, it costs money. Use the fan instead. Put it by my door."

"We'll call you after our first appointment."

He backs the car in rapid jerks. "What did you think?" he finally asks, accelerating down the empty street. The air is thick, like being underwater. Ella pushes the lever back to MAX.

"It's going to be hard. I feel so bad for her."

"I really want to take you to Key Largo—since we're here already. I want to take you to the coral reef; it's like nothing else you've ever seen."

"Hi. My name is Lisa, I'm Tammy's assistant. Please have a seat." David and Ella sink into plastic chairs before her desk.

"'Tammy?'" David has left his glasses in the car and squints to read the nameplate on the desk.

"Tammy's our assistant intake worker here at Carriage House." He wonders who is *not* an assistant; who, at the top of the command...

"As you may already know, Medicaid, in Florida, is a state program and is not necessarily applicable in all ACLF's."

He looks up quickly; he does not feel prepared. Back in California, in his mind, he'd felt prepared. He saw himself acquiring information, looking at facilities, then doing what had to be done—the paper work, the emotional work—then, somehow, moving on.

"I'm sorry. I don't understand."

"Adult Congregate Living Facility is short for nursing home."

Ella looks around the office: the calamine walls, the reproduction poster art in plexiglass, the plastic potted tree. David is explaining Lily's situation; and as he speaks, Lisa's patient fingers fold into themselves. Her coral nails stand out—ten perfect oval jewels. She wears her gold hair long; she is twenty-four, perhaps, or twenty-five. Just the right amount of shadow above her eyes—Ella thinks they're green; but perhaps she's wearing colored contacts and they're really some unimportant color—say, brown, or hazel.

"You'll need an application first. Then you'll need your mother's bank statements. You'll also need a letter from the bank declaring that she has 'x' amount of money in her account. Plus amounts of interest made to that account. You'll also need reports, and letters from her doctors..."

"I'm sorry, could you slow down?"

"You'll require proof of her citizenship, medical forms..."

"What would constitute proof of citizenship?"

"Birth certificate, passport, voter registration. We have lots of problems with elderly, especially women: many have no record of being born here, and in such cases Medicaid won't reimburse us for their care. We had a woman recently: she was ninety-two; she had no money. *We* believed she'd been born here, as her family said; but there was no proof, so what could we do?"

"Is there a long wait?"

"The wait is unpredictable."

"In what way?"

"How can I put this? Some months, everything goes fine; there are no vacant beds. Then you might have a flu epidemic that wipes out ten or fifteen people all at once."

"It depends on how many die. At any given time."

Lisa nods and checks her watch. "I'll show you the facility." They rise and follow her into the hall.

"I can't process all this information," David whispers.

Lisa points a finger to the dining room as the elevator doors snap shut behind them. There are eight communal tables in the room, yet the people scattered there all sit alone, as far from one another as the space permits. Lunch is an hour away, but the room can be used for other things, Lisa says, although she doesn't say what.

She walks briskly on ahead of them, her high sling-back heels clicking over polished floors, her cool green skirt switching side to side. They follow silently as she points to one room after the other, its use. The community room is small; in it, a herd of wheelchair-bound men and women are hunched in semicircle before a large color TV screen. Congressional hearings are in progress, but no one watches. The room is warm, a place to be. The TV is just background, David notes. The people stare out the window, or at the floor.

"This is the walk-in shower. The patients are bathed every other day: even-numbered rooms first, then odd."

"Every other day? I don't think my mother would like that."

"They can't be bathed each day, there aren't enough staff."

A scream echoes in the air behind them. Ella turns, but the corridor is empty, its bare floors shine. The cries accelerate; they're coming from somewhere down the hall, behind a large blond door. Lisa is explaining that at Carriage House, all attempts are made to separate the mentally confused from those who are alert but physically impaired. She doesn't break her pace, although the cries continue: a kind of keening—rhythmic, sharp, staccato; the pitch is high and piercing. It is human, Ella reasons; but it has exceeded human bounds. It's taken flight. It communicates as animals might, or birds— something in acute distress that has no language. *"Eee-eee-eee Eee-eee-eee Eee-eee-eee."*

"What you're hearing is an Alzheimer. She's not crying out because she's in need, but because crying out is a function of her disease." Lisa's coral lips spread back in confirmation.

Ella briefly catches David's eyes before he turns away. Lisa continues down the corridor, her hips swaying side to side, like a smooth young horse in spring. Crones in wheelchairs line the hallway here on either side; their fingers reach for her as she glides by. She nods to each, the way a queen might.

The nurses at the desk do not look up, although the cries continue. It is clear to Ella: no one plans to go to her; the large blond door is locked. *"Eee-eee-eee Eee-eee-eee Eee-eee-eee."* They're holding the elevator now; Lisa moves her arm in rapid strokes of invitation. As she hurries down the hall, Ella feels the thread between her and the woman break. But she hears something for the first time now: the way the cries respect the intervals between them. Her timing, those silences—as measurable as the spaces between notes. Perhaps she played an instrument once. And this is how it sounds—the last music that we make on earth before we go.

David leans against the pilings as the green Atlantic crashes at his feet.

"If we left early in the morning, we could see Key Largo and still be back by three o'clock."

Ella lies face down on the sand beside him, studying the variety of forms before her—every shell a different shape. Yet they share a common fate: to be deserted. Once, these structures housed a life. She wishes he'd lay off Key Largo; she hates the tropics, hates humidity and heat—and anything that could be thought a tourist sight. It's their fourth day. They have two more homes to visit, and the birthday dinner two nights from now. They're surviving this.

It wasn't hard to put the first home out of mind; they begin to blend. And their names—the way they're chosen to evoke the sense of elegance and privilege from another time and place: Manor House, Claridge Arms, Thornhill Green, Eden Glades, Idylwood Manor, Stonehaven. She has instructed her children: if she can speak but cannot walk, and she asks them to take her to the woods, they shouldn't question it. We all assume we'll have autonomy when this time comes; but it comes because we've lost it. She wonders if they'll forget their bargain then; if they'll do to her what she and David are about to do to Lily.

At the second home, only one thin arm reached out to her. It was just as they were leaving, and all the more surprising because she'd thought that they were clear. They were at the door, and almost out, when the woman's wheelchair stopped in front of her and blocked her path. The exit door was just beyond. She could see out through the little windows at the top: cars sliding up and down the avenue; the mall across the street; a woman with a baby carriage, strolling slowly in the sun. "Honey," the voice had rasped. The bony arm extended; the fingers were picking at her hip. Her eyes were spears, they stuck in you. "Oh, honey..." Those thin lips breaking into happiness at last. Such light was in her eyes—they've captured you; you knew it, there was no way out. You're her honey now.

On the morning of the unveiling, they assemble out in front of Lily's: David and Ella drive one car, taking Lily and her girl, Miranda, with the wheelchair in the trunk. Behind them, Jack and Poppy, their girl, Maria, and David's cousin, Allen, on his father's side, and Allen's mother, Helen, in the other. It is Allen's father, Michael, whose unveiling they will witness. The two cars hum along the freeway and it seems in no time they are standing in the cemetery, looking at the white cloth that covers Michael's plaque. He is in the top-row crypt of the out-door columbarium. The rabbi is in shirt-sleeves, sitting in his air-conditioned Honda, taking little drags off a filter cigarette. The family shuffles in the heat, and heads turn up expectantly —as though a window might be there beneath the cloth; as though this uncle will reveal himself in some unexpected way. Workmen labor next to them with jackhammers, breaking ground for another columbarium. The airport is next door and giant planes scream overhead to land. Miranda times them while they wait: four minutes in between. "I was on one once," she said. "To South Carolina. I took the Greyhound back."

Poppy stands beside her sister Lily's wheelchair; Miranda holds it steady with her long slim arms. Her dark skin shines against her pale green sleeveless dress.

"See, Poppy?" Lily points. "They discourage flowers here. The headstones are buried in the ground. Everything is neat and tidy." Her lower lip pauses, independent of the other.

Poppy leans on her cane and nods. "Yes. It's nice here."

Now the manager comes running down the hill to join them. He motions to the rabbi, who slips his jacket on and leaves the car. Just as he begins to speak, the jackhammers start up again and the manager rushes over to the site and holds up a hand for silence. When it is time to lift the cloth, a workman brings a ladder and climbs to where Uncle Michael waits. He reaches up and pulls the cloth down hard; it comes off easily in his hand.

Afterward, the women cluster in the shade of a thin young sapling near the curb, waiting for the men to bring the cars.

"Poppy. This is a nice place," Lily says again, reaching out to touch her sister's sleeve.

"Yes. It's very peaceful here." Poppy nods as the big jets scream above.

They have dinner later in a booth for eight. Their waitress, Rita, holds her pad and pencil poised; but when they order, her eyes just slip sideways, back and forth, like snakes. She repeats the orders slowly, many times.

"She's from Jamaica," Miranda says to Ella when she's gone. Miranda is from Cayman; she can tell where everyone is from: Jamaica, Haiti, Cuba, Puerto Rico. She hears it in their voices.

"Is she on something?" Ella asks.

"Heroin, most likely."

Afterward, they all drive back to Jack and Poppy's place for coffee. Somewhere on the way, David feels for Ella's hand; they clasp and hold, for perhaps a mile.

Miranda walks Lily slowly to a chair. She has left the folded wheelchair tipped against the kitchen wall. Lily tries to hold herself erect. When Poppy walks across the room, she eyes the polished cane and sighs, "I give her credit." She shifts her weight in the small, hard chair. "This damn leg," she spits.

"What's the matter?" David says quietly behind her. "What are you upset about?"

"I'm upset that I can't get around, that's what I'm upset about. I don't want to just sit around and become a fixture, if you know what I mean."

Poppy touches Ella's arm. "Come and see the ocean from the balcony."

"Tomorrow will be two years from the day that Harry died." Lily's voice is trembling. Miranda looks across the room at her and nods; her eyes grow dark and sad. Lily could be her mother, the one she left behind on Cayman Island.

"He always gave me roses. Tomorrow, when we visit him, I want to bring him two red roses. To represent the two of us."

The apartment air is cool; as Poppy slides the glass door shut behind them, Ella feels the heat. Poppy stands unmoving in the dark, one hand on the rail for balance. Ella leans over it. Fifteen floors below, she sees the patio, the lighted pool and lounge chairs. Beyond the sea wall lies the endless ocean, swelling in its inky blackness. The air is thick. High palms bend along the beach, shapely even in the dark. Tiny lights are blinking out at sea.

"Ever since we moved here twenty years ago, I've looked out there and known something," Poppy says. "See that curve in the distance? The curve of the sea? It's proof. Proof that the world is round." Her eyes are so triumphant, Ella hears the information as if it were a new discovery. Poppy gazes out to sea, swaying in the moist black breeze.

David leaps at the sound of the alarm. He reaches up to silence it, then falls back hard, an arm across his head. "I can't visit one more congregate."

"We still have Eden Glades. And in the afternoon, Shalom Gardens Memorial Park."

"I can't stand the way it wears you down." He stares up at the white whipped-plaster ceiling. "How will we get through this?"

"'One thing at a time—like a job,'" she quotes him.

"That's my mother up there in Bristol Towers. Going through this."

"Do you have the right directions?"

"I know where I'm going. The director said it would take a while."

Ella watches out the window, reading signs as the car weaves dreamily through unfamiliar streets. SINBAD MOTEL. VIBRATING WATERBEDS. MA-DONNA, SPIRITUAL ADVISOR. Between the grocery stores and laundromats, the grass is rich and green. High palms sway in unison above it.

"All those shades of green remind me of my childhood," David says, slowing the car. "It makes you think of names on crayons: Forest Green. Avocado. Lime. The way they used to smell inside the box."

"We turn right here, then left at the corner. That must be it." She reads the sign.

EDEN GLADES
AN ADULT-CARE CONCEPT

"They could have done without the barbed wire."

"That's not barbed wire, just a high fence," he says.

"They could have done without the armed guard."

"Maybe they couldn't."

The guard leans out the window of the little station. David rolls his window down.

"We have an appointment with Mrs. Stewart." The guard points left, toward Social Service.

"The grounds are huge—at least a city block." Aides in white weave in and out of doorways, swaying along the carefully planted paths.

The secretary says to wait; Mrs. Stewart is on the phone. Ella tips her chair against the wall as David takes some steps in one direction, then circles back again. The waiting room is small—a temporary wing while the new one's being built, the secretary explains. Ella notes the four large file boxes stacked beside the water cooler. She reads the label on the first, then turns away.

DECEASED A–J

1984

"What's the matter?" David whispers.

"Nothing." She shuts her eyes.

"Don't fade out on me now."

"I'm not; just resting." Her heart is pounding in the dark behind her eyelids. The elders cannot help us now; they have nothing more to give.

Mrs. Stewart leads them through the grounds. David likes her right away; a mature woman, for a change, with a realistic attitude. Ella watches his expressions: the way he smiled and raised his eyebrows in the Crafts Room. And in the Ice Cream Parlor, too. It was like something in a theme park: a young man jerking sodas behind a million-dollar lucite counter, while gray-haired girls in wheelchairs giggled in the back.

"My mother would love that," he'd said to Mrs. Stewart. But would Lily really love it, once the novelty wore off? How well can you disguise the last stop on the road? Lily's words are ringing in her head. "When you go into a home, that's the end of the line."

Mrs. Stewart indicates the forms she'll need from them to activate Lily's file, and points them down the hall and toward the turn they'll need to follow to the exit. Just before the turn, Ella sees the bulletin board with movable letters behind a nursing station.

This city is	MIAMI
The year is	1987
Today is	WEDNESDAY
Tomorrow is	THURSDAY
The next meal is	SUPPER
The weather is	CLOUDY

"What's the matter?" David turns as she reaches for his hand. "That's very practical," he finally says. "They get confused. It orients them."

They continue down the hall in silence. After awhile, he concludes, all these places are alike. At bottom. In the end. No matter how you dress it up. The same long corridors and double rooms on either side. Sometimes, you'll look in as you walk by; you know it's an invasion of their privacy, but you can't help it—your eyes just go in that direction. There's always an old woman in an oversized sweater, sitting on her bed and looking out at you. Or you'll make out a pair of legs—the rest's in shadow. Just a pair of old brown trousers, with legs inside them, lying on a dormitory bed. It's their room; and yet, it isn't. Tours go through here every day—and in the other places, too. He can't stand it, this one is the last he's going to see. He was wrong; people do *not* want a preview of their future, no matter what they say.

"This is not the way! I *know* the cemetery. This is not the way!"

"Mother, please calm down. I have to detour; there's *construction* going on. We'll get there. Don't be impatient."

Ella touches Lily's shoulder from the back seat, where she sits with Miranda. Two red roses lie in thin green paper in her lap. She stares down at them, anticipates their fate as sacrifices: lying on a marble stone and dying in the hot Miami sun.

"Harry! Harry!"

"Hold on, Lily," Miranda says. "He'll wait for you."

Two large tractors are widening the road, expanding Shalom Gardens. The foreman holds a hand up so the car can enter through the gate.

"Two more rows," Lily says. "Now stop. Stop here."

David and Miranda help her from the car and hold her up. Harry's plaque is two graves in. She has refused the chair. As her dead leg drags behind her, Ella bends to lift it with each step, pushing it gently into alignment with the other. David holds her right arm, Miranda has the other. Ella grips the roses with her other hand. The tractors grind their gears behind them; their baskets scrape the roadside, raising hot thick clouds of dust.

Lily stands before the grave, her light cream rayon dress twisting up around her body. Her left side tilts, beginning at her lower lip and moving down. Ella rolls the paper from the roses and puts one into Lily's hand. Harry's marker is a double. Over on the right, his name jumps out; the other side is smooth and uninscribed. Lily's standing at a slant between David and Miranda. Above her hand, the red bud curves down already in the heat—a tiny cane.

"He wasn't perfect," she begins. "But he was a wonderful man. When he couldn't do something good," she pauses, "he did nothing."

"Oh, Lily," Ella laughs, leaning into her. The rose slips out of Lily's hand and flops silently across his name. Ella lays the other next to it.

"Take your time," David says.

Then Lily finally shifts, and he and Miranda respond as one and turn her back in the direction of the car. Ella walks behind, lifting the stiff leg over the graves. Just before they reach the curb, Lily's heel catches on a marker and Ella bends to loosen it. The plaque beneath it flashes in the sun.

MURRAY   BETTY ROSE

TOGETHER FOREVER

Miranda waves from the end of the hall, and Ella shuts the door. She leans back against it, watching as David hunches at the kitchen table organizing Lily's papers. Lily is in the living room, curved in the folds of her orthopedic chair, a control switch in each hand: one to elevate the chair, one for switching channels on TV.

"Miranda's coming in the morning, to get you ready for your birthday dinner."

Lily looks up slowly, her eyes unfocused.

"You must be tired. Let me wheel you in the bedroom and get you ready for bed."

"No wheelchair! I can walk myself. With the walker. It takes time, sure; I'm not blind. But no. I can get around this place myself."

Ella draws a breath as she sets the walker in front of Lily's chair.

"It's the left leg that's the problem. It's dead. It won't come after the other. Have you ever heard of anything like that? It just lays there."

Ella holds the walker still as Lily grasps the bars. She lifts the left leg forward until it's even with the right. Lily takes another tiny step. They repeat this slow dance inch by inch. Lily loses balance once and pitches back, and Ella moves in fast to hold her up.

"I've had falls. But don't tell him."

"He knows you fall. The social worker calls him. He sees your doctor bills. That's why he thinks you would do better in a home."

"I will not go to a home. Don't you understand? I've been in those places, and believe me—you wouldn't want to know. They let you sit there in the hall. I was in one for a week, the time I fell. There was a woman who kept calling the attendants —she couldn't turn her chair around. Imagine, sitting in the hall alone, and no one coming. I called too, but no one heard me, either. Then I finally turned her chair around myself. I don't know how I did it, but I was mad. Here was their breakfast in that place: half a cup of cold coffee and a roll."

"Let me wheel you the rest of the way; it's late."

"No. I get around here on my own when you're not here; I can get around now."

"How do you get around when you're alone?" Ella feels the humidity flattening her hair; the slow ache that burns along her spine from bending down.

"I have ways."

"How's it going?" David calls. He's decided that it's simple, not complex, as he'd first believed. You want your life back, that's all. His eyes lift up from the bank statement before him. This is what you fear: the way it's all downhill from here. The way existence presses in and narrows.

"See, this foot just gives out on me. It won't do what it's

supposed to. You have to understand this, Ella: I will not allow myself to become one of those vegetables. I will not allow it. Look, I'll settle for twenty-five, thirty percent."

It has taken nearly twenty minutes and they're only at the bedroom door. Ella sees that getting to the bed will take another five. She can't bear the pace, its slow and torturous aim: to get from one room to the other. She can feel her impatience welling up, the threat of some wild impulse breaking through: to scream, take flight.

"I want the blue gown," Lily points as Ella lifts her on the bed. "It's over there—Miranda laid it out for me." Ella pulls the pale dress slowly from the heavy arms; slides the undergarments soundlessly down cold, veined legs. The blue gown slips like water on her shoulders as Ella guides the slow arms through.

"Back in 1938 when Harry's mother needed care, I quit my job immediately. I took her into our apartment and cared for her myself. She was grateful to her dying day. 'Look,' I said to her. 'You're my *mother-in-law*. Anyone would do the same.'"

Ella imagines it: giving up her job; lifting Lily up and down their stairs. "Things were different then," she says. Her words sound hollow, as do all the reasons why she can't do for Lily now as Lily did for Harry's mother then.

"The container for my teeth is in the bathroom." Ella hangs the dress inside the little closet. She moves on to the bathroom down the hall.

"I can't forget those women: no one came to visit them. You could see it in their faces. It was terrible, what can I say? When they sit there and see people coming to others, and nobody comes to them. I know what it's like in those places. I know what the outcome will be. It is not living. What can you look forward to?"

"Is this the one?" Ella calls, holding up the box.

"Yeah, that's the one, that's it. You know, Ella, I'm a simple person. I want to be an independent person, one with dignity."

"I know." Ella holds the plastic box as Lily fingers for her teeth, then drops them with a little click inside.

"I saw this program on TV: A man in a home who sat and never opened his mouth. Then some teenagers came to visit— it was a project for their school. They brought a little animal to him, and the man opened his mouth. It's amazing what it does for people. This man fondled it and talked to it. He came alive."

"If I were you, I'd want to stay in this apartment, too."

"Faye, she takes me over to the mall. They have K Mart and Winn-Dixie. I get around."

"You're very brave. I'd feel just as you do, Lily. I'd do just what you are doing."

"This gown's too short; I don't like the Baby Doll style. I don't know why I ever bought it."

The tall Miranda pushes Lily's wheelchair through the empty Hilton lounge. Poppy walks beside her, one hand on her cane, the other on Jack's arm. Minnie, Lily's friend downstairs, is on her other side. Cousin Allen guides his mother, Helen, slowly from behind. While Ella and David visited the home, Miranda washed and colored Lily's hair: champagne, with pale red tint. It curls softly and stands out from her face, the way a young girl's does.

"You look beautiful," Ella says, pinning a pale corsage to Lily's dress. A light lipstick coats her mouth; one side goes up, the other down—especially when she smiles.

"You think so?"

A thin blond hostess greets them when they reach the dining room. The dining room is empty, too. "It's off-season," David explains. He feels absurd announcing, "We have a reservation."

"For what time, sir?"

"For now. Six-thirty. Party of nine."

She shows them to a table near the empty dance floor. A lone waiter stands stiffly by.

"Take this wheelchair," Lily tells him sharply. She wants it out of sight, out of sight. This is her birthday. The Hilton. Her night.

"Watch my bag," she says to Ella as David prepares to guide her to her chair. "There's nothing in it, now. But still." It collapses in her lap—a silent thing from long ago, when she could shop.

The waiter brings a silver bucket for champagne that David ordered. He sets the fluted glasses down beside each plate.

"It's symbolic, Minnie," Ella says. "A toast to Lily."

"Oh, well, that's different. That's nice." Ella looks across at Lily, who is smiling faintly, as if she can't believe she's here. David is seated next to her.

"I want to toast my mother," he begins, and Lily's eyes begin to tear. "I'm proud to be here with you to celebrate your eightieth birthday." He leans to kiss her, then clinks her glass.

The waiter refills Ella's glass, then David's. The others stay untouched; their bubbles rise and rise.

The menus are bound in leather folders; the entrees run two pages. There is silence at the table as people study the selections, printed in medieval script. Behind them, sounds begin to fill the cocktail lounge. Ella turns and sees the notice on the wall.

RANDY
AT THE PIANO BAR

He sits before a synthesizer, pulling out the keyboard stops. The beat is dull. After drums and bass, he adds a horn, then violins and organ. His vocals, though, are live.

"You are the sunshine of my life, woo-woooo."

He sings it just like Stevie Wonder on the record, Ella

thinks, except his timing's off. He's very young, and blond, and yet it's clear he thinks he's Stevie Wonder. He cocks his head, in imitation, to the side. His eyes are closed, his lips are frozen back across his teeth.

"What's *he* trying to prove?" asks Lily.

David stares at Ella and nods toward Poppy, who sits beside her. *Help her with the menu,* he mouths.

"Have you decided what to have?" Ella leans, seeing her confusion. The waiter stands in back of Poppy's chair and waits.

"I'm not sure. I can't decide." She looks up, her eyes opaque. "I can't see too well; it's dark in here."

"I'll read them out for you," Ella says, beginning at the top.

"'STUFFED BREAST OF CHICKEN'

"'ROAST PRIME RIB AU JUS'

"'NEW YORK STEAK SUPREME'

"'VEAL CUTLET PARMIGIANA'

"'GIANT PRAWNS SCAMPI'

"'POACHED SALMON BEURRE BLANC SAUCE'" She pauses. "Anything sound good?"

"No . . . What's scampi?"

"That's prawns."

"No, no. I don't like that."

"'SHRIMP-STUFFED POMPANO'

"'VEAL PICCATA'"

"No . . . I don't like veal. I don't like fish."

"I'm having prawns," announces Lily. "It's been years since I had prawns."

"You are the sunshine of my life, woo-wooo."

"When is that man going to change his tune? He's been singing that for half an hour."

Ella drinks her third champagne. She looks across at Lily and starts to laugh. Lily giggles, too. "It's true!" she says. "He's boring!" Lily claims not to drink, but Ella notes her glass is now half empty.

"You're getting tipsy." David says, smiling.

"It doesn't take much to get me going," Lily gasps, then holds her side.

Ella turns back to Poppy. "Have you decided yet?"

"What's that, dear?"

"What you want to eat. Have you decided?"

"What are the choices?" Poppy's eyes drift down the table. Ella speaks slowly, omitting veal and fish, as well as foreign words.

"How about the NEW YORK STEAK?"

"Steak. No, I don't think I want steak." Ella looks at David. "Did you order wine?" she whispers.

"Yes. It's coming."

"Poppy."

"Yes, dear."

"I think the BREAST OF CHICKEN would be good."

"All right," Poppy answers slowly. "Yes, that would be nice. The . . ."

"BREAST OF CHICKEN," Ella tells the waiter.

By dessert, Randy has pulled some dance beats into play. When we were young, it seems the bands were older, Ella muses, watching him. Musicians at piano bars had silver hair. David walks around the table. "Come on," he whispers, pulling on her wrist. They step out quickly to the dance floor. Ella studies Randy's face: the little highlights on his cheeks and just above his pale blue eyes. Not a day past twenty-one, she thinks. When he looks at them, his lips curl farther back. He thinks they're all ridiculous. She's sure of it. She and David lock in step; his palm is warm against her back. She leans into him and shuts her eyes as the empty lounge engulfs them.

"We're driving to Key Largo in the morning. I've talked to her, she understands we need a break. We'll be back in time for dinner up at her place."

"We're the only people on the dance floor," Ella whispers.
"We're the only ones here who can still walk."

He accelerates the rented car. It's early; they'll have breakfast
in Key Largo. They should arrive within the hour. Ella watches
as the airport rushes by, and thinks how they'll be lifting off
from there tomorrow, before the sun is up. She imagines it: the
swift, thunderous levitation. Leaving all of this behind.

"Wait, you missed the exit . . ."

"Don't tell me how to drive!" he shouts. "I checked the map."

The tears leap up at last as she turns away and holds her
breath, imagining her second husband: what color hair he'll
have; his kind blue eyes. She feels the fingers wrap around her
arm.

"I didn't mean to shout. We've been under so much strain
this week. I want to take you to the coral reefs. I want to have
some fun before we leave."

"Good morning. We'll be cruising for an hour before we
reach the coral reefs. At that time, the ship will idle and you
will file downstairs to view the reef through special windows.
There's a snack bar on the upper deck, in front. Your first mate
is Kim and she will make announcements from time to time,
informing you of life along the reef."

David leans back, his feet braced against the rail, and sighs.
Ella leans against him sideways as the boat weaves slowly
through the narrow estuary toward the sea. Mangrove trees
cast tangled roots downward in the brine, catching the ebb and
flow of their wake. They are on the top deck, in the back,
where the sun is hottest. It feels good to sit and close his eyes.
He inhales the sea air, tilting his face to the sun, although he
knows it will burn quickly here. The waters lap the narrow
shore as the boat tips gently side to side. He breathes deeply to
relax, but his mind begins to dart from nursing home to nursing

home instead. He's shocked to realize the way they quickly blend. He can't distinguish one from the other now, only sees those hollow faces, the sea of failing flesh. Even the personnel —all the same: smooth, clean, management-trained. A young and healthy woman always smiles and greets you at the desk; and you smile back at her—out of some complicity, or fear. You both pretend that everything's okay. Those hungry eyes: you're torn between pity, and fear you'll soon be one of them. There is no middle ground. Their eyes crawl over you, as though seeing were their only weapon now. The old man in the wheelchair on the porch, the one who couldn't move—it was hard to tell: could he even hear the Benny Goodman in the speaker overhead? Could he dance it in his mind? You couldn't tell what stimuli got through, or if they even wanted it. Or whether they were, in some mysterious way, beyond the choice.

He shivers, even as the sun surrounds them—rebounding off the hot white deck and metal chairs. You go through life perceiving yourself as unique: you have your place, your friends, your identity as some *one*, who does some *thing*. Then suddenly, you're swept into a funnel where you're nothing once again. Plastic places, one after the other, filled with plastic people. He feels Ella's hand on his shoulder and jumps. His back is reddening in the steamy subtropical light. She rubs the lotion on in slow circular strokes, imagining they'll be together forever.

Speaking through a megaphone, Kim guides them toward the stairway to the lower deck, inside. It's dark and cool down here, and he is grateful for the change. The boat is idling now; the water on the reef is shallow—its bottom almost touches. Along the floor on either side are high glass windows: they press their faces close, as Kim instructs.

"Coral comes in many forms. Although it looks like underwater plants, it's really animal—a living being. It produces a stony, cuplike structure—an exoskeleton—into which it can withdraw. Over time, these skeletons build up and form the reefs. These are remnants of colonies formed after the Ice Age, representing coral that has died. Each generation leaves its skeleton intact, allowing new forms of life to move in."

Strange fish hover silently before them, just beyond the glass. Their iridescent skins flash in and out between the coral forms: rippling greens, and otherworldly blues he thinks could blind you if you looked too long.

"On your left, you'll see two angelfish," Kim announces as the boat begins to circle slowly and turn back. "Whenever you see angelfish, you'll see two of them together. This is because the angelfish mates for life."

"If we don't hit traffic going back, we'll just have time for a swim," David says, as the boat begins to pick up speed.

The beach is long and white, the breakers high. They step down quickly into slow green waves; it's always a surprise to her how warm these waters are, compared to the cool Pacific. They stand in water almost to their waists, their bodies moving with the motion of the surf. A sharp cry rends the air above them. A sea bird reels and circles there, tilting its small white form in arcs. *Eee eee eee*, its high thin cries echo far above the waves. She watches as it twists in the wind's crosscurrents, its beak locked open in alarm.

He dives inside a breaker at its thickest point—that ominous darkness at the center, just as it begins to rise. He disappears in it, then surfaces farther out. The next wave crests and washes over him.

"Don't go so far!" she calls, then follows after him. They ride the buoyant heights, salt spilling from their lips. They plunge through each wave as it comes to them. They could keep on swimming, beyond the curve of earth.

· · ·

At the deli on the way to Lily's, he waits in the Take-Out line as Ella double parks. She keeps the engine running, the air-conditioner on high. When they get to Bristol Towers, Lily's door is partway open; David holds the take-out boxes up and toes it open with his foot. They can hear the voices from the hall.

"Look, I don't have to tell you the story. You know the story."

"Lily, you have me. Even when I'm home, I think of you. I want to see you happy."

"Hi, everyone." He steps sideways past the pink Formica table and sets the boxes on the counter.

"David." Lily's voice is low, a whisper. "This is Luis. He helps me out."

David reaches out for Luis's hand. It's a strange sight: Luis sitting at the little table, his janitor's shirt rolled at the sleeves, the half-empty bottle of Bacardi next to him; and his mother in her housecoat at the other end, propped up like a doll on pillows in a green aluminum chair.

"And this is my daughter-in-law, Ella." Lily's face is slack, her eyes unfocused. David thinks, she's got the look already, she's one of them.

"Nice to meet you, Luis." Ella watches as he fills his glass again and knocks it back: he sees them as the kin from far away—who want to put her in a home. Unwilling to make sacrifices any decent folk would make.

"You're like my own mother, Lily," he says thickly. Lily's eyes slip slowly to the side, the way a schoolgirl's might. She's flushed, but Ella notes that the whole apartment's overheated. When she moves into the hall to turn the air-conditioner up, David follows, throwing her a puzzled look.

"He helps her out," she whispers. "He made those wooden bars along the wall so she won't fall." She gestures to the bars.

She smooths the tablecloth as David brings the serving dishes in.

"Luis is from Puerto Rico," Lily says as David squeezes past.

"Puerto Rico!" Luis echoes, banging the Bacardi bottle on the table twice.

"People tell me, 'Lily, you'd be better off in California.'"

"You need your *family!*" Luis shouts.

"Would you join us for dinner, Luis?" Ella asks.

"Thank you for asking me; but no, I have to go. My wife will wonder where I am. I look in on Lily. She needs someone to look after her. I do that."

"I know you do. It means a lot to her."

"I said to her, the social worker, 'What I saw there, God forgive me.'"

"I think your corsage has bitten the dust," Ella says as she flips the garbage lid down. "But the blue cockscomb will last; it's dried. It keeps its color."

Luis drains his glass and slowly rises, his thick hand spread for balance on the table. "I wish we could be like that flower," he says quietly, "and never die."

"We've picked the two best places," David says as Ella soaks the dishes in the sink. "We've narrowed it to two. You're on the waiting list at both—one here, and one in California. They're the only choices."

"I want to be with you. In California."

"We want you out there, too. But if the Miami home has an opening, you'll have to go there first. We'll do everything we can on our end."

"I don't wish it on anyone: to give up everything you own and go into a home. After a lifetime, to have to just fold up and say, So long, kid."

• • •

The motel is dark when they return; the outside lights are dimmed. The room, too, seems close—as though the air-conditioner had quit. The humidity is a presence, clinging to their skin as they pack. Just before she gets in bed, Ella throws the window open and pulls her nightgown off. The ocean is the only sound as it moves in, moves out. To the north, the city is stripped of light; the high-rises are dark, blending with the night.

"We made it," he says softly to the ceiling.

"She's so helpless. It makes me feel helpless, too."

"I know." He turns to her. He is weighted down with salt and heat. Dark waters pound against the sea wall, the air inside the room is thick and seamless as the night. He lies over her and they begin to blend, then burn as one. When she cries out, he whispers, "Yes." They're weightless, yet they're sinking, she can feel it. She spreads out under him the way she floats at sea.

The alarm goes off at five. The morning seems like night, although a storm has cooled the air. They pay the bill and step into the rented car for the last time. They ride silently on cushioned air through near-deserted streets that shine with rain. After check-in, he has coffee at the airport coffee bar; she waits in the lounge, with seven people lying on the floor who have missed a flight. The mother holds a sleeping baby in her arm.

The plane begins to taxi as a gray light fills the sky; rain beads it rows of windows. She stares out through the glass and sees the darkened palms against a pale horizon. This city is MIAMI. The weather is CLOUDY. She leans back and waits, her hand resting lightly over his. Something in her fights transition; you get used to things. She braces for the takeoff, as though gravity were all—that force that holds us to this world.

❧ YOU ARE HERE ❧

Arrivals and Departures

I USED TO WONDER how this family would end, what form that
end would take. The thought would surface in those height-
ened moments when the ordinary dailiness of life appeared to
pause, and a sudden dread descended in its place. An intima-
tion leaped out of it like a cold flash-forward to the future. It
wasn't always like that; in the beginning, I thought: This will
last forever.

It starts this way: Bread was in the oven, and I'd stepped out
into the night to cool and wait for it to rise; from the yard, I
heard the oven cracking with the sounds of its own heat. It was
January, and the air was smoky blue; a moon was straining to
rise above the house across the street. Branches from a storm
the day before littered the ground and snapped beneath my
feet. Through the next-door neighbor's window, I saw the pale

flicker of his TV. He was kneeling before it, as though in prayer: turning the knobs endlessly, trying to get what he wanted. The room jumped with harsh blue light, and as I watched, I realized that in the years they'd lived next door, I'd never seen his wife there watching, only him. She died in late November, her lungs collapsed from fifty years of smoke. I turned away and saw the moon lift over the roof of the house across the street. The people who lived there moved away in August, and the new family moved in last month. The windows still have the old curtains, though. I wrapped my arms around myself and remembered back to when we were the new family on the block. A plane droned east above me, toward New York, its tiny rows of lights like pinpoints in the haze. I imagined it as going back in time. It seemed strange—that people could sit in chairs in the sky; strange, that a plane could be sliding past the moon that way, almost touching.

I glanced at the old man again before I went back in. He's a toddler now; a woman minds him. It occurred to me then, in a terrible flash: we would be that way, too, someday. That early, I could see it coming. I saw it broadly, though, as fate: inevitable and slow. It wasn't imminent. It wouldn't be you.

The next time it happened was in June, when your parents flew to California for our girl's graduation. They had just arrived, that very night, when your mother slipped and fell. I thought: *It begins with them.* It was brave the way she waited for the ambulance, pulling little presents from her purse. When the doctor first confirmed the break, you were down in X-ray waiting for the slides; this was when I saw your father cry. He was speaking of the couple in the apartment just below them: how they'd withdrawn their life savings; how they'd finally risked it all to take a special cruise. But two days out, he'd had a stroke. "Just when they could have a little something," your father said, stressing the "little something" as though it were the least that could be expected from a life—that one small thing. He lit another Winston as his eyes refilled. We waited as the doctor led you to the viewer by the nurses' station to see your mother's X-rays, which had just come down. We watched through the partition as he snapped the switch behind the screen and slid her film in place; the white light flickered there and held. You bent together, looking at the break. It seemed so strange from where I sat: that you could see your mother's pelvis, lit from within; that you could stare that way, into the source of your being.

All that month your father paced the house, a cigarette between his fingers, wondering what to do without her so far away from home. For the first time, I understood that we are prisoners of this flesh.

"Let me call the senior center—they have programs in the afternoon."

"I'm okay, I'm okay," he'd say, hitting out another Winston.

I phoned the center anyway.

"'Chinese breathing'?" he repeated. "I *know* how to breathe!" He began to cough.

"They have Dream Therapy and Aquapeutics, too."

"Leave me alone!" he cried, his frail hand cutting the lines of smoke, his voice breaking.

I called the center back. "Don't you have bingo, or cards? He's a simple man."

"No one has to come here if he doesn't wish," the lady said.

We visited the hospital each day, and watched the Democratic convention in the evening. Jesse Jackson was saying, "Time is neutral and does not change things." But he was wrong.

Our girl's graduation came and went. We hardly noticed, with so much to do. When your mother could finally travel back, we were already into summer. They sat together under the Departures sign while I went to get them coffee. She was in a wheelchair by the boarding ramp, clutching her purse in her lap. We sat together quietly and didn't speak; by then, there was nothing left to say. I thought: They are about to fly back, into their past; into time that has already been. It was not until the freeway, driving home, that I finally thought of us, our past. It was our beginning, once; it was all arrivals then.

That first Christmas, when I came back from Canada by train—we'd just begun; we weren't even lovers yet. When floods washed out the tracks, I had to spend the night in Portland; my seatmate from Vancouver shared the room. It was a strange sensation—gripping the receiver of the pay phone in the hallway of the Y, as your number buzzed and buzzed—as though wanting to confirm that something there was waiting to be born. We had only met, and already I thought this: He's out with someone else. I stopped trying sometime after midnight. The girl from Vancouver didn't even wake; but in the morning, she said, "They're all alike." And then the next train came and we were on our way again. We sat together, swaying back and forth; she drank a Coke and read a movie magazine. I stroked the collar of my coat and thought of someone else.

The next night, as the train slid smoothly to a stop, I peered out through the window at the station, just in case; but you weren't there. I gathered up my things and waved good-bye— she was staying on until L.A. I swung my suitcase down the platform and fell in step behind the crowd. The night was cold. I was looking for a cab when you tapped me on the shoulder. You were behind me all the time.

By September I was thinking of our girl: how she was almost grown, how it had gone so fast. I knew it was in the order of things to let go, and that knowledge didn't help. I kept seeing her as she was then: when she had just arrived; and your arms already reaching toward her, before the nurse was fully in the room. You wrapped yourself around her and began to rock. She lay there on your knees—forming an O with her mouth and locking her eyes on you. "O, O, O," you whispered back to her. Those were your first words.

The day she left for college, traffic was light; even on the road, it was hard to believe we were finally on our way. I told myself: *We still have our boy.* He sat in back with her, his feet up on a suitcase, a transistor in his ear. You were in the front with me, sleeping against the door, your fatigue an extra presence among us. We were four hours late from your first nap. Signs along the road whipped by. WALNUTS NEXT EXIT. APPLES ONE MILE. I had the volume low on an oldies station that had just begun to fade. Shirley and Lee were singing, "Come on, baby, let the good times roll," and I was tapping my foot to the beat, remembering how we had danced to this once, as though we would go on forever. Now it's the future already, that time is gone. Cars cut in front, each bumper sticker different, yet the same. I ♡ CHIHUAHUAS. I ♡ JESUS.

"Why is Dad so tired," she asked.

"I don't know," I said, squinting into the distance ahead.

"He slept all day," she whispered. SUNSTREAM HOMES, FROM $99,999. RENT A GLIDER—EXPERIENCE SOARING.

She wanted to postpone the dorm, the last good-byes; so I pulled into a lot to park. We could explore the campus first. You didn't stir—not even when I bumped the concrete marker with the wheel; you just shifted your position and settled back into the same sleep. *Come on, baby.* The kids walked slowly on ahead while I coaxed you back. "We're here?" you said, your green eyes widening. We walked along a path beneath the trees and you said "What's the hurry?" twice, so I slowed my pace to yours. The leaves above us were still green; it wasn't fall here yet. They cast heavy shadows on the grass. It reminded us of when we'd started out like this. "I feel I'm going to college again myself," you said. The air was hot and still, the way it gets before a storm. We walked slowly now, our arms were crossed in back. The landscape stretched before us, wide and unfamiliar. It was Sunday, everything was closed. We passed some buildings, but they weren't marked; they didn't say Art, or Biology, things you'd expect. We felt disoriented by the time we reached the mall. There were empty picnic tables there, and wooden benches on their sides. Over by the darkened bookstore, something large stood out and caught our eye—those maps that orient you when you're lost. We clustered in front of them, squinting at the colored networks, more confused than ever. A thick red arrow pricked a small blue dot and signaled YOU ARE HERE. I stared, my reflexes dulled by the heat, my mind repeating, *We are here. We are here.* As points of reference, the dot and arrow meant nothing—just pretty symbols, afloat in unmarked space. But I knew this: we had come to this point in our lives. We were here.

The Colors Just Before Night

When we left her, she was oddly calm—as people are before accepting some unfamiliar fate. "Take care, Dad; please get better soon." Your arms encircled her and held. I stood back as you embraced, your bodies fused—as though a single entity were being lost to me. Youthful forms swirled around the dorm, surrounding it. We waved good-bye, and she backed slowly into that swift stream and was absorbed. I turned the wheel sharply, pointing the car out into the coming night. The sky above the campus was a filtered lavender. By the time we reached the freeway, heading west, all the colors changed: the deepening rose of the setting sun, the orange and silver clouds around it, the purple night—behind us now, but gaining.

Our boy sank deeply in the back, folded in the silence of its space. You leaned against the door again and shut your eyes. "Don't worry, honey," you'd said to her as you embraced. "I go for tests tomorrow; it will be nothing, you'll see." The hum of the wheels as we accelerated down the concrete strip/the black hills erupting on the western rim/the long night turning blue-black from behind—everything blurred, as though we were taking off. For one blinding moment, I experienced soaring.

K Y A *Remembers*

Now I'm on the seventh floor, looking out the window through the evening haze, staring at the old clinic building just across the street. We are here again, where everything began: the hospital where we first met, and where the children first arrived. Behind me, a nurse is helping you in bed; she tears the cellophane from the lid of your supply tub and arranges your things on a table. I can't take my eyes off our old building; it is not the clinic anymore—that's gone, that time is gone. They had a party at the end, to honor all the years of teaching and service to the community, before the cutbacks closed it down for good. Some people were depressed and couldn't come; but many did, dressing up in cocktail clothes, determined to forget this was a wake. You made an effort to have fun that night, to suspend the knowledge that a portion of your life was ending there. The planning committee had rented the Academy of Science; we passed slowly through the wide glass doors, and it was pure hallucination after that.

A punk band was hitting it, hard and loud, beside the alligator pit. People in long lines were snaking, doubling back, their shoes slithering over terra-cotta tiles beside the bar. From your place in line you could see the alligators just below you, their crusty skins half in, half out, their thick tails low in the water, covering the pennies; their slow eyes staring hard. Behind them, in glassed-in cages in the wall, coiled snakes raised their heads even though it was night, and slowly rocked from side to side in trances as the beat thundered over cold floors and metal rails; when you finally reached the bar you had to scream to be heard.

Beyond the alligator pit, the bar, the band, were darkened hallways stretching for what seemed like miles, their black walls lined with tanks of colored fish, lighted from within. They cast an eerie glow on people flowing through: dark suits, shiny gowns, transparent glasses held up high. When you reached the end, the space expanded—opening up to show a long buffet that stretched across the porpoise tank for its whole length: it was just a wall of solid glass, filled with water, where the porpoise chooses between plunging down; rising to surface; or propelling across. The trip across is over in seconds, so it would alternate: belly up; then down. I studied its face and wondered if its perpetual smile were an evolutionary trick designed to hide grief; and whether alligators, underneath, were kind.

The caterers could not keep up; they were bending over tiny rounds of bread, arranging caviar on top, while people scooped up three or four at once and swallowed them whole. You couldn't reach the table no matter how long you waited. I drifted in the crowds inside the darkened passageways, where people I knew seemed like strangers, and I passed them by. The band's noise penetrated, even here; I leaned against the wall and closed my eyes as though to shut out sound, imagining the green-haired guitarist in his frenzy tripping backward on the rail and plunging into the alligator's stony jaws. The walls pulsed with life; the way it stared out at you when you stood before it made you short of breath. Anemones opened and closed in the artificial tide-pool room as people dribbled drinks across the carpet; lizards blinked in unexpected afternoons. Night and day reversed themselves, and it seemed this wake would never stop; that every creature moving blindly through these labyrinths, or trapped inside, was waiting—breathless, in confusion, for something to end.

Now, from this height, the clinic seems innocent of history: a boarded-up shell. But we were young once, inside it; we had dreams. "Don't worry," I hear him saying now, "it will be all right." I hear the scraping sounds the nurse makes in the bathroom—kicking the flip-lid pail in place, attaching a fresh curtain in the shower. "Everything points to kidneys," the internist says, reviewing the test results. Far beyond the clinic, a lighted billboard rises in the night: Superman flies inside it, advertising something I can't read from here—just the words in the balloon above his mouth: I'LL SAVE YOU.

"We've scheduled other tests; the specialist will be in tomorrow. We'll have to wait and see." He sits down on the bed, his fingers knitting in and out, his manner kind—unlike a doctor. "Mother Nature throws us curves," he said, and that is when I knew. When I kiss your lips, your eyes don't close. The hall outside your room is my destination now.

Going down, the elevator stops on 3; two orderlies push a gurney in from ICU. The doors snap shut and we descend. I'm between the wall and the man on the gurney: his mouth hangs open and his eyes are closed. He is mostly tubes now, his face is the color of gravel. The orderlies discuss some party where they got wasted. I think the man is dead, but they don't notice. When the doors open up on 1, I stand sideways and slide out first. The lobby is cold, the furniture, deserted.

Driving home, the bay stands out—its glassy strangeness like something undeclared. The lights of the city rise up out of the darkness. My index finger feels along the dashboard for the radio and pushes—hitting 1960, the year we met. Old familiar voices reach out through the night. *You set the world on fi-ah. You are my one de-siah.* I imagine him back there on the seventh floor, staring at the ceiling, reliving his history; while here, inside the car, I'm reliving mine, with him. My hips move with the beat, even sitting, with one foot on the pedal. *Baby, baby, please don't leave me.* YOU'RE TUNED TO K Y A¡ GOLDEN OLDIES EVERY DAY¡ RAMA LAMA DING DONG FOREVER¡ HEY, HEY, HEY¡ KAAAAY WYYYYY AAAAAY¡ THE BEAT GOES ON¡ K Y A REMEMBERS¡ I turn the volume up as high as it will go. *Oh, no, not MY baby; oh, no, not my sweet baby.* The lane ahead is clear all the way to the tunnel. I'm on automatic now. *Bye, bye, love. Bye, bye, hap-piness. Hell-o loneliness. I think I'm gonna cry-ee.*

Saving You

"It comes on suddenly; we don't know why," the new doctor explains. His phrase was, "out of the blue." My phrase as I stare at his desk is, "neat as a pin." This is the first of the conferences, the only one where he is still patient and I am still polite. Fear can do that; you make some kind of bargain, without knowing: if you're calm—asking the right questions in a serious manner, not slouching in your chair—some chink in the wall will be found and you'll slip through. "It doesn't look good. If the inflammation can't be stopped, the damage is irreversible. Then there's dialysis; but we're not there yet."

"It's serious," I say when I phone our girl at college. Her

brother knew from the beginning, because he was here.

"Why did you wait so long to tell me?" she cries, as though betrayed.

"So you could get settled there, before you had to come back here."

"I understand your motives," she says, blowing her nose. "But don't ever do it again. He's my *father*."

I drive to the hospital in the city each night after dinner; I still have my boy, and he goes with me. The first night, he sat in the chair beside his father's bed, the sports page open on his lap. They talked about the Giants, but the subject quickly exhausted itself and they fell into a fragile silence. The sound was off on the overhead TV, but the picture flickered near the ceiling; it seemed to pull your eyes in its direction no matter how you resisted. The bed was cranked partway up and he lay in it, bent at the middle, his slack hands on the sheet in unnatural repose. He was wearing the light blue L.L. Bean pajamas from last Christmas. When he finally turned from the TV, he noticed the pale tears sliding down his son's face. "Come here," he whispered, reaching out to him. They embraced, then held; then lay together, sobbing as one. I gathered up the papers that had fallen to the floor.

When she arrives on Greyhound, it's as though she'd never left; as though, if he weren't in the hospital, it was the same old family, doing the same old things. The new tests are in, the diagnosis confirmed.

"I feel terrible," the doctor says. "It's not going well." Prednisone is all he has to give. He tells me how terrible he feels; and when he speaks, it resonates inside my head like sounds inside a chamber. "I feel terrible" *terrible terrible terrible.* "He's getting worse." *Don't say nothin'/bad about my baby.*

I push the button now and ride to 7, where he lies semiconscious under sheets, his face distorted from the drug. I stroke his forehead and he whispers, "Is it really darkest before dawn?" When I drive her to the Greyhound station Monday morning before the sun is up, wasted men are spitting on the sidewalk out in front, as though it were still night.

I can't stand his face, his nervous hands, meticulous desk. "No, no, no, a Chinese doctor can *not* treat him in the hospital. It's against the rules." I push the Xeroxed article across the desk and say, "This indicates a statistically significant improvement in the patients treated with both Western and traditional Chinese methods."

"This research was done in Shanghai," he says, flipping to the summary. He might have been saying, "This research was done on Mars."

"Look," he says, dropping the article soundlessly on the desk. "Destroyed tissue does not regenerate. His kidneys will not come back" *come back come back*. I rise from the chair and reach for the article. I go out through the waiting room and down the elevator and onto the street. The school of Oriental Medicine is five blocks away. I walk quickly up the hill and pause in front, waiting for my breath to slow. When I ring the rusted bell an iron gate opens. It clicks behind me as I climb the narrow stairway to the second floor. The air is close; it presses in and has a musty odor that I can't define—like something dark and brown that keeps to itself. How do I begin this? What do I say?

A receptionist steps forward and I ask for the director. The article is rolled tightly in my hand. He comes toward me down a darkened hall and bows as we shake hands. I explain; the air is hot. I take large breaths to get enough. He doesn't move, but when I stop he says, "We must know each other long time, then you trust me and I trust you." I try to breathe from below. I watch the papers shake as I offer them to him. "This article says herbs must be given with the other medications; timing is essential. His tissues will be dead within three weeks. There isn't time for us to know each other." He glances at the article and nods. "Then take him to Shanghai," he says.

"He can't leave the hospital. Can you refer me to someone else?" I watch his quiet eyes. They are not ruthless, nor are they kind.

"We must know each other," he repeats, and bows. If my knees buckled, and I sank without a sound, would he prescribe a remedy for that?

"Thank you," I say, and turn away.

Running down the narrow stairs, I feel his tissues burning— like something that is fried; they curl up and grow hard.

In the street, the air is cool, impartial—like a weatherless day. Superman still floats inside the billboard at the bottom of the hill, the empty promise on his lips.

What People Can Give

The doctor phones again. "We've put him on dialysis; we have to get the poisons out." I watch as the receiver moves slowly back in place. I am not connected to it, or to him. I try to imagine what dialysis is like, but nothing comes to mind. *You are there. I am here.* The phone rings even as I'm watching it. A friend relates a nightmare he had the night before: "I was running from these mysterious things behind me. I was trying to get away, but they were always there. I couldn't shake them —no matter how fast I ran; I'd turn around and they'd still be there, hanging on, the way that little kids do." I say, "kidneys," and there is silence on the other end. "We'll come over with a pizza around six." I say, "Okay." "Then we'll go to the hospital together."

We still have the dessert a neighbor left this morning. People are strange, the ways they give: some are there for you when you need them most, and couldn't ask; others you expected, disappear. Some send flowers, and you never hear from them again. Some bring food, but do not stay; others stay, but do not eat. The phone rings and rings; you try to be polite, because they care. Sometimes my mind will drift. I think, First you are alone, and then you love. The love is lost, and you're alone again. You survive alone, and sometimes you will love again and sometimes you never do.

The doctor calls again. "I don't want to alarm you," he begins, "but we had to transfuse him. He's in intensive care; I want him watched while we do more tests."

I put the receiver down, but don't remove my hand. Who should I call? Who would come, and what could they do? It rings again, beneath my hand.

"What kind of pizza do you want?"

"He's in intensive care; they think he has an ulcer, too."

"We're coming. We love you. Is mushroom and green pepper okay?"

It is night; ICU. I go in alone, glancing sideways down the rows of beds. I marvel that people look like this and still survive. When I reach his place, I see a plastic trash bag on the counter with his possessions twisted up inside. I see his pen, appointment book, a tie, the L.L. Bean pajamas. The bag's collapsed, as though he were silenced there inside. I go around the bed and take it in at once—the bloodless face, the bloated form, the yards of tubing, his open mouth crying without sound in the sterile light. I wonder, How can he look like this and not be dead? I take his hand, but there is no response; nothing moves, nothing comes back.

One Brief Hour

It's October now. I bring him colored leaves I gather on my morning run. I keep running. He should have something natural, even a leaf. Around midmorning, I pause from work; out the window, I see the winged termites erupting through cracks in the ground, fluttering on wings they just grew, rising in the air in unison, like a sheet. It happens every fall like this: they struggle from the earth, usually after rain, and fill the air— flickering slowly up into their brief lives. Their wings are thin as paper; they flash like tiny mirrors, attracting the birds. In moments, they are pecking away, throwing their beaks back to swallow. It happens so fast; an hour later, all you see is wings, like tissues, stuck to the pavement. In one brief hour, they're gone.

As Though Through Rain

Our boy has trouble concentrating now. I leave a message for his teachers in the office. We all agree that she should stay in school up there. She can come on Greyhound in emergencies. I'm still trying to save the kidneys, in spite of what the doctor says. At our last conference, a friend came with me. We sat together, facing him, and from across the desk we heard his fate. "Look," he said, brushing invisible lint from his sleeve, "it's been nearly a month and nothing has changed. There's no point kidding ourselves about this." It was like overhearing something about someone that you weren't supposed to hear; or, hearing, didn't want to know. It was all the worse because the person didn't know it, just lay there sleeping under sheets. "Are you saying it's hopeless?" I asked, as I stared him down. "We never say things are hopeless," he said.

Afterward, the friend and I had lunch. We sat at a small table and ordered wine, our fear for him a new bond between us. I began to feel like an ordinary person: eating a meal, drinking a drink, having a conversation. Later, when the wine was gone, he ran his fingers through his hair and said, "I feel terrible; we're here having fun, and he's in there." Later still, I lay awake, my heart hurting in strange ways, and begged the darkness: Don't take this away. It was like a new life; I could imagine living it. I wondered: if it is understood that life leaves much to be desired, why do we go on desiring?

He's back on 7 now, a different room. All the flowers from September died; I had to throw them out. At the end of the conference, just as we were leaving, I'd asked him straight: "If you think the kidneys are dead, why are you keeping him on drugs?" He said, "We do everything we can. We have to play it out." I play it out in Chinatown. I have a new address and this time I'm hanging on; it was on a piece of paper and I lost it once before—somewhere down on Sutter, or back in the garage. The doctor's name stayed in my mind, though, and I went into the Hyatt to look the address up again. The rain was coming hard and at a slant; my hair was soaked and lying flat when I finally reached the lobby and started looking for the phones. Polished women with fine skin and dry shoes slid soundlessly over carpets; somewhere a cocktail piano was playing. I imagined a darkened room filled with lovers bending over little flames. The pay phones were beside the reservation desk, and that's where I saw the calendar and noticed the date with a shock—those numbers framed in brass: 10/18, the day we met, our unacknowledged anniversary. I heard dance music starting in another room, and thought how, at this moment, his blood was moving slowly through a cold machine; and how I would soon be running through the streets of Chinatown, looking for a doctor who could give back what he'd lost. We could be here, drinking cool champagne, moving in the room where music was, our bodies giving off light. We could be remembering how it felt to be new in the world together. I looked around the lobby for someone to begin with once again, imagining that sweet tension, the unexpected possibilities, and something inside me broke, but did not come apart.

I'm walking fast down Stockton, glancing into herb shops, wondering if the answer lies inside: that perfect substance that will make the kidneys live again, and bring him from the brink. The streets are dark and wet. The clinic's in the basement of a building I can't find. I stare into the faces in the crowds, catching their guarded eyes under black umbrellas. I finally see the sign, just inside a narrow alley; the English part reads: ENJOY THE BEST IN ACUPUNCTURE HERE! And on the building opposite, another sign, beneath a second-story window: FURNISHED ROOM. If I crossed over, I could go up those stairs; I could disappear into the furnished room, and that would be it: a new life.

In the waiting room, a teenage girl stands up behind a counter and offers me a clipboard with a form. Her teeth are whiter than her coat and she wears a fuchsia lipstick on her lips. I wait standing; I stare into the color TV. The guy is saying, "I know about you and Steve, Diana; but I understand. Your life was torn apart, you wanted a new life." And she is saying, "I didn't want a new life, Roger! I wanted my old life back. I wanted you!"

The doctor is polite; he stands before me, bowing slightly, and I bow slightly too; it just happens. We face each other in front of the TV while I try to explain what I need. Diana hurls herself in Roger's arms, and now he's holding her. He whispers soothing things. I have to speak over his voice as the girl in the fuschia lipstick looks on. The doctor finally says, "I look in library for kidney. I send you something when I find."

That night, he phones to say he dreamed of me. I haven't dreamed of him. But waking once, at 2 A.M., I had a vision: him on the pillow beside me, as before. Everything I see or hear is polarized—experienced with blinding clarity; or blurred, as though through rain—as things look underwater when you're sinking.

Uncharted Waters

Every other day they send someone up to 7 with a wheel-chair to take him to dialysis. He sits there quietly, his hands lifeless in his lap, like someone else. I kiss him, though, and watch him disappear around the corner down the hall; but I don't go down with him. The first time, I was alone on 7, it was night. His room was empty and the nurse looked in a chart and said, "They're bringing him up now," but he didn't come. First, I organized the flowers: pulling out the dead ones and throwing them in the flip-lid can; then I watered the azaleas and chrysanthemums, pinching off the withered buds. I smoothed the bed and read *The New York Times*, then stood be-fore the darkened window and watched the night. An hour passed that way. When I couldn't stand it anymore, I went back out and asked: if they were bringing him up an hour ago, why wasn't he here? You hesitate, because you don't want the answer. She consulted the chart again, then telephoned down. We waited as she listened, and everything on 7 seemed suspended—as though the sound on all the TVs had suddenly gone out. "He's left," she said, and at that very moment I saw the gurney rolling toward me down the hall, two orderlies on either side. In the center was a mound, that's all; it wasn't him. It took three of them to transfer him to the bed; he couldn't cooperate. His body shook, as though it had faulty wiring. He reached out to me and cried, and when I took him in my arms, his flesh felt chilled, as though he'd been refrigerated. They all stood back and waited. Later, when he was finally sleeping, the nurse looked straight at me and smiled. "How are *you?*" she whispered softly. *you? you? you?*

I have another address in my pocket, and this one might be it. We spoke briefly on the phone, and I'm driving down tomorrow for a conference. I felt connection as we talked—a kind of understanding. When he spoke of energies and inner harmony, it didn't sound like hippie talk, but the real thing. And it isn't just because my other leads are gone; I really think this may be it. His office is way out past the airport, down in San Mateo, but what is distance? It's true that time's been lost, but I can't dwell on that. It's true he's still on 7, but the doctor said it himself: they're treating him conservatively, and if he doesn't bleed internally again, he might come home.

It's November now, the leaves are gone. He couldn't appreciate them. They just dried up and had to be thrown out: useless, out of context. The conference with the herbalist went well. His office smelled of pepsin. Herbs inside glass jars lined the walls in rows. "Five thousand years of trial and error," he grinned, pointing to the herbs. "The ones who didn't die, we keep those herbs." I said I'd bring him in as soon as he could leave the hospital. But later, on the freeway, I lost heart. He's just winging it, I thought, and pushed the button fast. *Shoo-be-doo-be-doo-be* DO DA DAY. I sped past the airport with the volume up. Weren't we all winging it? How else were we surviving?

There was congestion just before the city and I switched lanes in anticipation; but most of the time it doesn't do much good. You might shave off minutes that way, and often your choice is right. But sometimes things will shift; it can surprise you. I'm a prisoner of this car; it responds to every touch. It drinks the air ahead, its wheels purring. When the lyrics on one station make me short of breath, I just push the button for another. I've put four thousand miles on since he got sick; I look directly at the toll takers now, meeting their eyes. *I get around, round-round-round, I get around.*

We have made it to Thanksgiving; he is home. We are all together now, back where we belong. We celebrate with friends who were there for us when we were going down, falling through the hole that's made when gravity implodes. Someone puts a record on and I get up to dance. He's been home three days; he mostly lies and sits. When he looks up from the table, his eyes are his again. The candles warm the surface of his face, smoothing what he's been through. I smile at him and gesture that he join me. It's a slow and haunting rumba, in a minor key. He rises now to meet it, making his way back to me. He tries a little step, although his face is slack, his movements slow; we aren't touching yet. He is looking at his feet as he concentrates on the step. I think, *soon we will be as before.* Now we lock together lightly; his hand is warm again. We start moving slowly with the beat until it seems a part of us in some mysterious way. We move in place and close our eyes. The music seems to hold us there. I feel it move inside me now, creating what it most resembles: an ecstasy and sadness that seem almost the same thing. We give ourselves to it as though there might be something beyond this loss. But before it ends, I'm falling into his frail arms. All the places in me that didn't move before are opening all at once. Holding our position, we step slowly out the door as the music plays for others still inside the house. I lean away from him, above the cold garden, but he holds on. He whispers, "Love," his name for me. We cling, although I broke the rhythm. We hold each other up as our breath sends urgent signals in the night.

We're driving back again, before the sun is up. From the bridge, I see the freighters scattered on the bay, their dark forms anchored on pale water, like toys. He had chills last night and shook. Holding him made me shake, too, and eventually I turned away. Traffic is light, we'll get there early. "Are you scared?" I ask, parking beside the curb. He nods. "A little." I hold his hand and watch the nurses arriving one by one, from several directions, for the seven o'clock shift. A boy walks by tilting, his radio big as a suitcase, his leather collar up. "Endurance is all that's left," I say, as the street lights flicker off. An abstraction; yet it is what we do. We were driving on the coast at twilight once and saw a large brown rabbit by the road; our headlights illuminated its eyes. It wasn't dark yet, you could see it clearly, hunched stiffly in the grass. It didn't spring off, the way they usually do. It was still there the next morning, only on its side: stiff, already blending.

We take the stairs together slowly; my arm is linked through his. He grasps the rail and pulls away, and my arm slides out. "I can do this by myself," he says, stepping faster now to prove it. I follow, down a corridor of closed steel doors; this unit used to be something else before it was this. The walls are green, the air smells cold—like wet cement. He pulls a closed door open, struggling with its weight, and then we step inside. I take it in: the dark machines; the nurses' station in the center; the black recliner chairs along the walls with tiny TVs mounted on their arms. He takes his sweater off and hangs it slowly on a hanger with the others. I stare at all the empty jackets, sweaters, coats, as though each waited for a spirit to return. A nurse helps him to his chair. I look at her, but not the people on machines. She says this chair is "his"; he has it every time. The old man next to him has fallen to the side; he drifts there, breathing through his mouth as a game show crackles on his tiny screen. The motor whirrs as his machine whisks blood through the needle in his arm; I see it looping there inside transparent tubes. When my baby rolls his sleeve and the nurse inserts his needle, I think I'll scream, but don't. "I'll be back for you at seven," I say clearly, as I kiss him on the lips. We've made it to November and he is still alive; you work with what you're given.

When I return, I suggest the Chinese restaurant up the street. "Is this symbolic?" he asks quickly. "To prepare me for the herbs?" His doctor warned me last October: "Your hardest task will be convincing *him*." So I sat beside his bed and said, "We must consider everything." He didn't interrupt; and when I stopped, some brief intensity flared behind his eyes, no longer than a second, and he simply said, "I love you," and I took that for his answer. Election night, he'd bled inside again, but didn't say a thing. Ronald Reagan's face was rosy, like a baby's; but his was cold: the bottom of a river where it's shallow. The doctor said, "We avoid the operation if we can—we give transfusions first." I watched the dark blood falling slowly through the tubing to his arm and wondered who it came from, and whether they had AIDS. This was when I first began to think of life in

terms of probability; it was just another perspective, and perspective helps us survive. I noticed a pattern then: first, there's
fear; then some adaptation.

We are swinging up the overpass again. My mouth is dry.
This time, this is it. He collapsed this morning, the minute he
got up. "I couldn't stand, that's all; it's nothing," he is whispering now. He is slumped beside me, but I look straight ahead
and not at him. We crest the elevated off-ramp and I see the
frozen sea of cars before us, eight lanes, stretching all the way
across the bridge to San Francisco. I go cold. "Just keep driving!" he says, sinking farther down. I look ahead, behind, and
to the sides, but we're surrounded. A film runs through my
mind at thirteen frames a second, faster than Chaplin: I am
standing on the car roof, waving my arms as though I might lift
off. I scream for help, but the film is silent, the wind just
snatches it away. And then I see a distant object in the sky. He
is flying swiftly toward us now with outstretched arms, his cape
is floating over the silent cars.

He leans on the counter in Admitting, waiting for the volunteer to take him up to 7. "Did you bring my warm pajamas?"
He is shaking. "I need my warm pajamas!" he repeats. "Can't
you see I'm *cold?*" We stumble to the elevator and the doors
snap shut at last. The volunteer taps 7 and whistles absently as
we go up. I hold my breath and watch the numbers flash.
Behind us, something's sliding to the floor. "It's all right," he
whispers weakly from his knees. "It's not all right!" I scream,
going down with him. Then the doors snap open and we hurry
down the hall, one of us on either side of him. We are shown a
room, and help him into bed. He lies there staring at the ceiling and I walk slowly to the window to inspect the view. There
are two: the one to the south, and the one to the north; these
small variations have begun to interest me. "Are you feeling

better?" I ask as I stare out. "I'm fine," he says, resigned to what's ahead.

A nurse blows in, her shoes squeaking with each step. She pulls a chair up by his bed and hugs the clipboard on her lap.

"Oh, not again," he says. "I was just *here*. Check my chart. I've done this form before."

She draws her knees together. "I'm sorry, but we have to do this every time."

He doesn't want to be unkind; he struggles on the narrow bed. "You're not going to ask my hobbies again."

"Yes." Her red lips tighten. "You have to answer all the questions on the sheet."

"Okay, okay." He winks at me. But when she gets to "Hobbies," he says, "I don't know," and I suppress a laugh. She flushes. "I have to ask your hobbies, and you have to give an answer."

"You have no right to ask irrelevant questions," I finally say. "He's bleeding internally, leave him alone."

"All our patients are sick," she snaps, cementing herself to the chair.

"Why does this hospital need to know his hobbies?" I persist. He lies quietly now, his skin like cold pebbles.

"So when the Bookmobile comes by, if his hobby is reading, they know to stop at his room."

"Fishing," he says finally. "Baseball, dancing, jazz."

"What time's your first appointment?" he asks me when she leaves. He looks quickly at his watch. "Get something to eat and go. I'll have the doctor call you later. I'll be all right." I sit on the bed's thin edge and lower myself down on him; his cheek is cool on mine. "How can you stand this?" I whisper into the soft ear.

"I don't know," he whispers back. His hand moves up and down my back. "How can *you* stand it?"

"I can't." *'Cause baby, it's you.*

• • •

Crossing the bridge again, the city melting behind me in the haze, it's as if pieces of our lives are breaking off, lifting into the current that flows to the past and is lost. And I think: if it were a simple thing to find myself in uncharted waters, I could feel my way by the stars above; or, if all were blackness, sense my course by the tilt of the sea, its rise and fall. But this is beyond navigation. I am entering space, its cold regions; that black velocity where windless currents circle and collide, stealing my breath as they go.

Night Engravings

The phone rings in my office just at five; the doctor says, "We'll operate within the hour."

"I can't stand seeing Dad that way again," my boy says, his voice breaking. "I understand," I whisper as I hold him. "So will Dad." I ride with friends this time. I sink into their back seat, and start to shake. It should be a relief not to have to watch the road; but now I see that watching helps. It takes you out of certain realms.

We push the button and ride to ICU, on 3. There are couches, coffee, and a large TV. They wait as I go through the doors. I move slowly, afraid of what I'll see. Tubes run from his nostrils and empty into something behind the bed. Even with the morphine, the contractions make him scream. He grips my hand and waits. "I'm so relieved it's over," he finally says.

The friends go after me; the rule is two at a time. I wait for them by the TV, where colored forms are moving back and forth. I can't hear the sound, although the sound is on. When we finally go back down, the elevator doesn't shake from side to side as much, the way it does from 7; it doesn't have as far to go.

It's late when we get back. The friends step from the car and embrace me on the sidewalk. It's a paradox: that you're most warmed by holding when you're already warm; there is a kind of coldness so in need of holding, no embrace could reach it though it held forever.

It's clear tonight, the air at twilight like high thin bells. I have the radio silent; there's a visual music out there, playing on the silver blackness of the water. Even the battleships have a kind of beauty. I see the city rising in the rose-gray air, its buildings filled with tiny lights, their dark shapes etched against the sky, and I know that all of this will come back again someday, standing out like permanent pictures of this time. Everything I see as I wait for him is held in that suspension: the city that contains him—its black, uneven outline fixed forever now, as though engraved on night.

I walk down the hall, over polished floors, through the ICU. He's not where he was last night; someone points: he's on the other side, behind a glass partition. I go in alone. Machines behind him blink and beep and suck. He's taped all over, wrapped in tubes; but this body isn't his: it's twice his size, and seems to hover over the sheets, floating like a figure in Macy's Thanksgiving Day parade, with a dummy's face on top—gargantuan, with slits for eyes. The bile tube streams away, flowing to some unseen place. *You are here.* I bend to him and whisper, "I AM HERE." Through some night, he struggles to respond. I take his swollen hand; the ring is gone, sealed inside an envelope in the cashier's office safe. I speak in whispers to the air. The bed is high, the one chair low. I reach up to the form that lies there now, but can't embrace it. Knowing that I knew it once sustains me. "Can you talk?" I say, and wait. He

makes a sound of pain. His swollen fingers wrap around my
hand, then fall away. He can't see me from behind those eyes. I
sit in darkness with the hand; it's my connection. I rest my
head against the metal rail that's up so he won't fall, and think
the only thing that's possible to think: Body is all—that physi-
cal presence that represents us in the world.

It's late. I'm chilled and start to shake, but I don't want to
leave him here alone. Every time he comes here, I fight the
thought he won't come out. I have a permanent pain from this,
in the place where wishbones are on turkeys; as though a
breath were taken long ago and not released. I wonder: do we
fall in love with forms? Or the spirit within? I try again to reach
him, but he floats in transit now, between worlds. He's no
longer himself, but some replica meant to stand in—as though
a part of him were splitting off, preparing to say good-bye. I
lean into him and try to bring it back. I go down now, to the
ear; it's an avenue. I say, "I AM HERE." And I say, "I love you, I
AM HERE." There is no sign, but I keep talking, fighting this
departure with speech. This is like a death, but I am talking
into the tunnel, stalling it. *Be my, be my baby. Be my baby now.* In
that viscous dark interior the twin kidneys flicker for the last
time. I lean across the bed, still holding the cold hand. I am
learning to forget the kidneys: their time, their possibilities. All
I want now is his face, transfused with someone else's blood.
Saying to me the things he says.

The elevator wraps around me and descends. It's warm inside. I hold my breath as we land, waiting for the doors to
open. It's close to midnight now. The lobby is deserted; the
plastic couches, bare. The overhead fluorescents cast a bluish
light. Through the automatic doors, I see the dark, unpopu-
lated night outside. Behind the information counter, a watch-
man reads the paper. There's a walkie-talkie in his pocket. I see
the light above the pay phone on the wall; I walk to it and lean
my elbows on the little shelf below. I want to call someone, but

imagine everyone asleep. My fingers wrap around the black receiver, but do not lift it off. *Well, here it comes. Here comes the night.*

Crossing the bridge again, traffic is light. In the mirror I see the city rise behind me in the blackness, darker now, its windows dimmed. Gladys Knight is singing, *Every road has got to lead somewhere, we've come to the end of our road.* There are times I'll have the thought: I haven't lived. I think everyone wants more of it, and measures this by what hasn't been, rather than what has. And when I think this of him now, it comes as a surprise: that this has been the life. We have lived it all along.

When I get home, my son's asleep. By now, I'm wide awake. I am thinking of his grandparents, the way we saw them from a distance—not without compassion; but seeing how they mostly lived in pain, we'd think, They live with pain, it's theirs. I get in bed, but do not sleep. I turn and face the wall, and this is when I understand that heartache is not a symbolic condition. I do not cry, I wail—like Ronnie and the Daytonas. *Wa-Waaa wa-wa-wa wa-wa Waaa.*

In the morning, he pours his cereal slowly in the bowl. I don't know what to tell him now, so I just say, "Dad is getting better. You can see him soon." He had a dream last night. "Dad was in it. He said, 'Farewell.'" "That won't happen," I whisper. "He'll be all right."

They think he's getting better; there is only one thing wrong. When he speaks now, it's in circles that lead nowhere. He smiles, but there's a hollow quickness to it. His gestures are abrupt; twice, while scratching, he pulled out tubes and had to call the nurse. "Slow down," I say, affecting calm. "What are you talking about?" he snaps. He tosses the newspaper onto the chair and misses. "I'm just fine. Very rapid recovery. I'll be out of here by Monday." His eyes dart around the room, seeking something that isn't there. He stretches out his arm and points: "Hand me that," he says quickly. His hand twitches as he waits. He sleeps all day and listens to KJAZ in the night. "I don't want to go back to normal sleep," he said. "I think a change is coming." And then his head dropped back, he fell immediately asleep.

We're in December now. Sometimes I sit with him while he's asleep, looking out the window at the view to the north: white buildings, stacked upon the hills like blocks; cumulus vapors arching above them, like dreams. And I think: there are forms of despair so deep that over time it's transformed into something different—say, desire. I lift his cover; I no longer care about the tubes. The bed is narrow, your body strange now, not your own. Someone else's blood is moving in your veins; you're no longer you, but I still know you, I know you. I burrow into your body, calling to whoever is there. I AM HERE. You stare up, your new eyes blank. Nothing comes back to me. But I'm finding it again, discovering the places where there are no incisions. You almost see me and remember; but then your eyes fall back into themselves and leave me on this shore. I lie over you in desperation. Your skin beneath my hands is smooth, warmer than the heat at the center of the earth. *Baby, baby.* I'm circling now, I press down hard and hold you. When you finally speak, I look up in surprise. "I think in bubbles," you say thickly. "There goes one now. . ." You reach for it, clicking your tongue as you snatch the air.

The conference starts on time. We sit together facing him again across the immaculate desk; the friend is talking now. He listens tensely, his beady eyes on us, his hands clasped underneath his chin. I stare at the cufflinks that hold his white sleeves together, the black hairs on his wrists. The friend is saying, "These drugs are making him crazy; how much longer will this go on?" "It's not the drugs," he answers quickly, as he lifts a ballpoint pen. "I think it's emotional," he adds significantly—as though he were an expert, and this a finding. He twirls the pen between his hands. I meet his eyes. "Of course it's emotional; that's what those drugs *do*—make you crazy emotionally." My voice has an edge; this is where things break down. "It isn't drugs," he says sharply, tapping the pen on the desk. My heart misses some beats. And then I say, "If you're right, then he has brain damage from the blood loss." I step off into space. "I've discussed that with the surgeon," he says quickly. "And we both agree: that didn't happen. There is nothing physically wrong."

Afterward, we go to lunch again: the same table, same wine, the same desire rising up out of the dim light. "I think he's nuts," he finally says, referring to the doctor. "You said it," I say, catching the waiter's eye and pointing to my empty glass. "This must be unbearable for you," he says, his eyes on me.

"I'm still here," I say; then look around, as though to check. I don't define where "here" is. The difference between where he is now, and where I am, is that I can come and go. When I am *there* with him, it reminds me of Antarctica, although I've never been. I've seen pictures, though: vast mountains, sheets of continental ice, chill waters, strange light, forms of life that cannot speak. When I am HERE, I want only to dance, if dancing means to couple and to live. Everywhere I drive now, that's the message.

We're at the corner now; we go our separate ways. "Hold on," he says, as we embrace. I'm here now; I lean into him and hold. When people say that, it's usually metaphoric—as though thin air were adequate support. Sometimes, I think this: that we were put on earth to comfort one another; it's the only explanation—an afterthought, some final consolation.

I bring him soup in a Thermos, but he brushes it aside and shakes his head. "I might be leaving on a minute's notice." It's the ninth day; there are no new theories. "We have to withdraw him slowly," is all the doctor says. I lie over him, avoiding the scar, and cry into the pale shoulder. YOU ARE THERE. I AM HERE. When there is no response, I rise. "I'll call tonight," I say, as I move slowly toward the door. His hands rest immobile on his gown. I go down the hall to the elevators and push the button. One and 7 are my numbers now. When the doors finally part on 1, I turn right this time instead of left, toward the cashier's window. I am taking back his ring. "I'll need two pieces of I.D.," the woman says behind the glass.

That night I write some letters with his pen; I wear his ring. Now that he's in outer space, we communicate by phone. We speak briefly of the children, then the conversation stops. He starts humming on the other end, a melody from some old forties song. "That's an old song from an old time," I say, and there is silence. "I long for a simpler world," he finally says. "When I still had my kidneys." Before I can respond, he says, "I'm very sleepy now," and then the line goes dead.

The next day he refuses calls, and won't call out. He just lies curled up beneath the sheets; if anyone approaches, he pulls farther down. When I try to phone his room at night, the switchboard intercepts it. "The patient don't wish to be disturbed at this time," the operator says. I plead with her to put me through. "I'm his wife," I say. "I'm sorry, ma'am, we're not allowed to do that if the patient don't desire it." *desire it desire it.*

I phone a friend, but he says, "I'll go back when he's himself." I wait, my breathing hard, wanting, from the bottom of things, a resolution. "There is nothing we can do," he finally says, his own voice breaking. "It's a dog's life." Then I throw back my head and howl, but it isn't crying anymore. I double over and it seems I'm crazy—the laughing will never stop. It releases me; I know I've heard the truth. This must be the answer I've been seeking all along.

That night, I enter sleep as though it were itself a dream. I am in an elevator that is rising and descending; it sways wildly, side to side, bumping the walls of the shaft. I push all the buttons on the panel, but the panel has gone dead. I pull the emergency lever, but it breaks off in my hand. It dangles from a spring that's coiled loosely, like intestines. I can see inside the hole it made—it's dark and viscous, like the inside of a body. I grab the phone to call for help, and a voice instructs me kindly: try this knob, or that. I say I've tried them all and everything has come apart. The voice is the only connection now. I could rise and fall forever, with only the voice for comfort; but I know it, too, will lose its power in time and there will be only silence, and this wild, continuous falling, until the ropes and pulleys fray and finally snap, and the elevator plunges down to darkness.

Phases of the Moon

It's mid-December now, people are thinking of Christmas. Driving him home this time was like the others: he sat staring through the windshield straight ahead, his hands curled in his lap like dead birds. Each time is like beginning again. I played every song on the air that night, pushing all the buttons, trying to get a response—I even cheated at the end and inserted a tape. *We can face the music, together,* the voice on it sang. The moon was sliding low in the west's black depths. I pushed Repeat and accelerated onto the bridge. *We can face the music, together, dancing in the dark.* On the other side of the tunnel, he spoke for the first time. "Is that some kind of message?"

The walls of the dialysis unit hum, maintaining life. Behind a curtain, an old man loses control. Nurses rush to him, making it right. I'm sitting on a plastic chair against the wall, waiting for the doctor to come out. He has a new infection this time, and they're examining him again. The doctor walks toward me slapping his stethoscope from hand to hand. "If you want some great food," he says, "they're having a Christmas party in the lounge." The odor of the old man's accident hangs in the air, but he doesn't seem to notice this. "They've got a great spread," he continues, spreading those hands to indicate its breadth. I stare up at him in disbelief; can't he see we're going under? I'm about to say something sharp so *he'll* feel cut, and it comes to me: maybe he just wants to dance. Why should he be exempt?

This time he's only in a week. I visit in the evenings, but occasionally at dawn. Even the roads are all predictable by now: every rise a known thing. Driving over to bring him home again, I crest the incline before the bridge and there, in the western sky, I see it going down: the pale, slivered curve of moon. Already I can imagine its thin shadow sifting to dust over the dark Pacific.

The first night back he shakes with chills. The herbs were supposed to adjust this, although they failed to save the kidneys; but nothing works so far. The herbalist had even put a needle in his ear, explaining, "It's called Gate of Heaven." By this time, I was thinking: all of this is something put in motion long ago, and now we have to play it out. Driving back, I tried to joke: "He gives good Gate of Heaven." The herbs sat quietly on the back seat in small white bags. The freeway was a sheet of rain, and cold, like metal. Later, when the herbs had boiled an hour, I drained the liquid out for him to drink. They lay there withered in their dark brown juices, vitiated, no longer potent. I peered into the container: they're nothing but debris, what you step on when you're walking in the forest after rain.

When he sleeps, it is as though I am alone. I wake often: even the half moon seems blinding at those times. There was a dream in which he said, *We are done with that forever now,* and I turned away in sorrow; and turning, saw an open window, and beyond it, rolling waters of another time. I saw animals there, shining and strange, walking the ocean's floor. Perhaps it was part of Pangaea, that continent a million years ago: a piece that was torn from the mass and, grieving, fell under the sea, pulling its creatures down with it. They were not amphibians; they were mammals. I thought: they inhabit those depths, yet they do not die.

When I wake, I hear the sound of rivers rushing, but it's just his arm beneath my ear; the mysterious blood seeking its places again, going where it goes. I see the half moon tilting, almost down, a fading shell. And then I sense you moving toward me in the darkness, moving through the stages of death, treading water thick and black. I feel you coming, working your way back to me. You're moving now, you're here, just as before. When I look again, the moon is gone.

It's January now. As I run around the lake, my breath collects before me in the winter air. It's early morning, yet the moon still hangs suspended in the western sky, its north side torn away. A dim light pulses from within, burning through the bronze smog like some relic from an ancient time. The pelicans are out, looking for fish, feeding among the Styrofoam cups and abandoned carts that break the water's surface like strange growth. The egrets, too, are here, rising from the water on legs like pencils, their purity untouched. She's gone back to college now, that's where she belongs. Other runners circle and repeat, but I just go around once; we recognize each other now, and sometimes wave. In the distance, an unfamiliar form moves slowly toward me, bent so low it looks deformed. As we close the space between us, I see it's an old woman trying awkwardly to run. My first thought is, *She's old;* the second, *I'm not there.* Just before we pass, I see her twisted face, her wool cap falling at a slant, the hair escaping from beneath it in bursts

of ragged whiteness. She holds arthritic hands in front of her
—the way a boxer would. I think: what impels her? What is
there to gain?

I'm nearing the end of my circle, rounding the park on the
north. I look out across the water as I slow my pace. The
pelicans are rising from its scummy surface, tilting their proud
beaks back as they have always done. I stare at them, surprised,
as though it were an unfamiliar instinct to know that all is lost,
and still go on.

LETTERS
❦ TO THE DARKNESS ❧

I
Things Passing into History

W HY should this be hard? It's a simple story—of things
passing into history.

There are cycles to everything. First, you're born.

It starts with family—the earliest thing you know. Later,
when you step out into the world, you think you've left it
behind; but it sticks by your side. It takes up residency within.
It expands there, growing large. You could have sworn you
were alone.

Years pass; and one day you find yourself back in that co-
coon: THE FAMILY, the tightest enclosure in the world. You
think you're starting over, but it's all the same—the one inside,
the one without. You're the hub of this one now, its center and
its pulse. You feed it and it thrives.

The years keep passing, but you're absorbed; you hardly notice. You look back from time to time, comparing what you

have with what you thought you'd have. You understand the split between dream and reality; the tension that split creates. In time, perhaps you say: You can't live more than one life well; and eventually, you decide. You aim for that one thing— call it happiness. It can come when you least expect it, although you worked for it; and when it comes, it's often not what you had thought of as being "it." It's usually something ordinary—a thing so simple, you look back afterward and think: That was it? and laugh.

Later, things happen. It can come apart in seconds. Imagine this: Someone taps you on the shoulder and says, "Your future is over." Just like that.

When you were the hub, you'd think: *that will never happen.* You were so proud of all you had achieved. The house is dark now. Things happen; people change. Life as we once knew it is over and will never come again.

Back in the beginning, he said, Would you like to come with me? and you said, no. Later, he said, Will you come with me now? and you said, maybe. This was the beginning, Bunny Berigan playing, "I Can't Get Started With You." He loved the sound of horns. Finally, he just said, Come with me; by then, you smiled and went with him.

When the girl was born, he held her facing him and said, "I can't believe she's ours."

When the boy arrived, he searched the tiny face and said, "He has my eyes."

He's on life support now. And you are staring into darkness, learning the limits of fear. You've lost him, but he's not gone. It doesn't matter where you turn, what you're seeking isn't here. Voices whisper from old regions in your brain, and you invoke them all: lovers, parents, friends; you'd go back to ancestors, if you knew their names. You call the names you know, but they return to you as echoes. Slowly, the way you'd feel along a wall, you begin to address the dark directly. It has no face, but it has presence. Soon, it will engulf you, you'll be one. In the meantime, you tell it everything you know.

You say: I built a life, and now it's gone. You jump at the strangeness of your own voice. A friend, speaking once of books, said this: "It's possible to transfer intact what's in one mind to the mind of another." Now you think: If I could speak, I would transfer this pain to someone else; then it would be there, and not with me.

Some nights, the darkness is so thick, the boundaries blur and you're almost synonymous. It begins this way: First, you think: if you could just try harder, you'd find a way to bring him back. If you reach far enough into that space within, you'll find a way to bring him back to life. For if he lives, he will be himself; and if he is himself, you will see yourself again, in him.

You've heard it a million times, the expression, "not himself."

When he was himself, he loved you. He moved with you through the common life you shaped. Now he's neither alive nor dead, but in some state that has no name. On bad days, it seems clear: he's dead—but it hasn't hit him yet.

If he were just reduced, and yet himself, you could bear this. You would learn all the avenues in the new, reduced world and travel there with him.

The boy put it this way: "There's a void in him, a coldness. It makes you feel you don't exist."

I am thinking of being elsewhere.

You return to the house, but its walls cry out from the weight of all those pictures: our images, everywhere—histories of a life. I can't go near the large one: all those arms, encircling. The way we fold into each other, and become a unit. Us, as we once were. I don't look.

This house was filled with LAUGHTER once. The garden

hummed with MUSIC. At the center were the CHILDREN, and our FRIENDS. We thought we would live within that world FOREVER. It was our LIFE. This house was filled with LOVE. Even when we fought, love was the CENTER to which we all returned.

Now the house is DARK, the garden filled with LEAVES. You twist the key and step inside. The air is COLD. You look around the room and think: This house is DEAD. My home is GONE. Our pictures line the walls—an exhibition. Our spirits hover in the vacuum of its space.

"This won't go away," the doctor said.

It stays with us, now. It has moved in.

The night is dark. He is alone. You are alone, elsewhere in the house. You enter his room, looking for something. His voice floats out of the darkness. "I miss you," it calls out. You slide down beside him. "I miss you badly," you whisper as the stone fills your throat again. You're a crying machine now, you never stop—except in traffic.

You're walking down a road. It goes on and on, it stretches to infinity. You admire things along the way, sometimes you linger for years. You know the infinity point will someday be reached, that it's inevitable. You don't think of it often, but when you do it's always the same size—a dot on the horizon. It has to do with distance, not with you. You walk and walk, then suddenly a door appears before you—up against your face: that close. Why do people say they never see it coming when it's right against your face, you think, your heart racing, stepping back as it swallows you whole.

Or you can be out walking after rain. The night is coming on. You look at all the houses—those boxes of light; and the gathering of forms within, glimpsed between the curtains as you pass. Other lives, warmly lived. You, long ago. This is the old neighborhood, the small apartment where it all began. The yellow leaves are pinned on asphalt by the rain. All is like a dream: the mists of night, the pale high moon, the flickering street lamps, our old window—disembodied now, just another square of light. From that window, you first imagined the long history that is now behind you; imagined it as future, then. You can sense the old bed just beneath it; the first child stirring to be born.

This was your philosophy: that what happened didn't matter, but how you met it. Now you know: What happens matters; it can break you.

This is how you think now—in clichés. Imagine that someone came up to you *in broad daylight*, and tapped you on the shoulder. *Out of the blue*, he said: "THIS IS IT."

It's Saturday again; a silence settles over everything. You're thinking of people in restaurants, holding hands across small tables. He's back in that place, underneath thin sheets. You are just a trace to him now, someone who weeps inconveniently in the night.

You wake at four, curled in his space, breathing his scent on the pillow, remembering you loved him once. You think of all that was good in him, and might return.

Last month, his weakness lifted briefly, and he came to you with flowers in his hand—as though he were your old sweetie once again. He did a little jig as he held them out to you. You looked up in surprise. "You're feeling good again," you said. "Don't question it," he said, and quickly fell asleep.

When he went away, you thought: the future is that outer ring we never see, suspended in interior space, always out of reach. The other night, you bumped each other accidentally in the hall and then held on. You bang your heads against this thing, not knowing what to do. You still reach out, though;

you're all you have. You continue the forms. When his frail arms wrap around you out of habit, you don't resist. You'd take anything, even a shell.

All that's left is loving him, and knowing that you can't—and the tension this creates. To love him is to share his fate. Straddling these states is like stepping into sunlight, then shadow, before the night comes on.

It feels like this: First there is the self; then the NOT SELF. You speak to him, but he won't look up. Or: you begin to cry, and he'll look into your eyes and say, "What's wrong with *you?*" His eyes are not like eyes; they're like things that were inserted in some factory—beads they put in toys.

In the beginning, we lay together. In the beginning, his eyes were ribbons of mesmerized light.

"He doesn't treat you like a human anymore," the boy says, shedding angry tears. "Don't say that," you beg. You have to think it first yourself, so you won't be caught off guard.

"It's chilling when he looks right through you."

"Not another word!"

When everyone's asleep, I tell the darkness everything. *Darkness, don't refuse me, hear my plea.*

When he's asleep, he sometimes shakes and sometimes screams. His mind begins to slip its boundaries, like spilled ink. This is when you rein him in—the way you would a spooked horse. You whisper, "It's all right." That's the hard part.

Or imagine it this way: as though it happened somewhere else—say, Argentina. He is taken in the night and kept *incommunicado.* He's gone two years. During this time he's tortured—twice to the point of death.

Later, he's returned to you, but not as himself. You struggle to recognize him, and fail. You perceive it as your task to restore to him some state you cannot name; but you are failing in this, too. You know this, though: You can't live with terror indefinitely; one day you'll defect.

When things are bad, I drive. I pull out into the night, burning off the miles between us, as though I could leave it all behind. I'll wait till dark. It's almost the same as addressing you: all blackness and no answers.

I like a wide windshield—the way it admits the sky. Rushing through the wasted landscape, the tape deck loud: some nights it almost seems a substitute for closeness. And congestion is a challenge: you bypass first; then cut in. It takes coordination. If you judged character by bumper signs, you'd be confused. I BRAKE FOR ORGASMS. I ♡ ALL LIFE. DIVERS DO IT DEEPER. EAT BERTHA'S MUSSELS. Even restaurants speak directly now: WELCOME ALWAYS OPEN. Sometimes there's drama. For example, the man on 80-westbound, just the other night. He's in the fast lane now, and I'm behind him. He's gesticulating wildly inside his silver car, screaming at the girl beside him. He doesn't stop for eighty miles and I'm behind him all the way—except for once, when I pulled abreast to see the girl. She's blond, so young. You want to take her home and teach her to respect herself. She's impassive; her eyes stare straight ahead and do not blink. He screams, she listens. She holds the same expression, then they exit at Pinole. He never hits her. And he drives well, even though both hands are off the wheel.

At the tollgate, there's a jam. A motorcycle crowds my lane, but I just wave him on. He signals thanks and then I smile—as though this were a true encounter. It brings to mind the man in the garage: We were underground, and waiting for the elevator in the fumes on Level 4. He had his Chow dog on a leash. We stood before the button panel, waiting for the doors to open. After a certain time had passed, I bent down to admire the dog;

it seemed inhuman to be standing there so close without acknowledgment. The dog gazed kindly up; its coat was burnished orange. The man warmed up in a cold kind of way, as though speaking stretched the limits of his nature. In a slow, meticulous voice he explained the origins of Chows in ancient China. He said their value there was thought to lie in imperfection, rather than a symmetry of coloring or feature. "Their beauty can't be obvious," he said. "There has to be some flaw."

This time he's cut in three new places. When he wakes, he says, "It would be better if I died. I'm just dragging you down with me."

If I drive fast, I can forget. I have a full tank, clean windshield, and high hopes. The dusk is lavender now; it hums on the horizon, as though time had finally stopped. A neon sign is etched against it, some unobtainable promise held within its bands of thin red light. I'm cruising now. The purple night, the low black hills, streak by. As I approach the banked on-ramp up ahead, I perceive it as a thing of beauty—its curve and calibration: something in its angle makes you want to claim it, to drive fast while tilting on your side.

We're at the bank, sitting in plush chairs, waiting for a clerk. The line is slow, and he's impatient. I say, "Just relax." My breath seems stuck within me; I can feel it stalling there, so I know I'm really speaking to myself. "Don't tell me what to do!" he screams. His parka slides off the chair and crumples on the floor. Some people glance our way. High up on the wall, behind the clerks, a Silent Radio is flicking out the news in moving beads of light: CURES PAIN . . . RESEARCHERS CLAIM STUDIES SHOW EATING MACKEREL, HERRING, AND SARDINES AND OTHER FOODS LOW IN POLYUNSATURATED FATS CAN RELIEVE MIGRAINE . . . INFLAMED

JOINTS... AND OTHER FORMS OF PAIN...

COME BACK TO ME... I telegraph, but all is silence. I whisper it again, and aim directly for his eyes—the dark spots at their centers—but the message falls into them and drowns.

People say, "Hang on." I think it means, Don't let go.

In the afternoons, he sleeps, drifting on a low hum, through the barking dogs, the fading light, the lurch of day toward evening. His sleeping fills the house the way that air expands balloons, inflating it beyond its boundaries to the point of pain.

I'm walking through the rooms again. A family lived here once. It used to be a home. I created here for others what I most desired myself. The rooms are just containers now.

I could flow out here forever on the river of night. It's hard when you come to red lights—the way you have to wait there idling, the cars around you tuned to different stations.

The western fog is moving low, in sheets, across the ridge—illuminated from within, like pearls. Someone on KTIM is singing, "I saw you last night and got that old feeling." I get the old feeling, hearing it. Then Benny Goodman starts playing "After You've Gone," and I suck in all the air I can and hold it, praying that the lights stay green. Behind me lies the history of our life together, all those accretions of incident and expectation. I call to him, down that long tunnel: COME BACK TO ME. But there is no response, just blackness stretching the length of it.

Darkness, you were always there. I tried to leave you, heading onto the freeway as though it were a way to be free. I tried to run away, but love seemed to hold me here with him. Eventually, I turned around. I told myself: you have to see him through THIS. But THIS could last forever. I eat the miles the way his tiredness eats our hours and days. GET UP! OR STAY DOWN! my Silent Radio screams. MAKE UP YOUR MIND!

He can not rise, but he won't GIVE UP THE GHOST. He just lies there now, his mouth spilling colorless lines of saliva on the pillow. I imagine burning everything after he's gone, a purification: his spirit will release into the smoke and find its new home.

Darkness, I turn to you again—the way, last night, he turned to me. He came to me for holding; he had chest pains and he couldn't breathe. You know this bed, left over from another time: so narrow, the first time we made love here, he said the only way it could support two bodies would be vertically. That was back in the beginning. Now, we sleep in different beds, in different rooms, on different floors: we've gone that far. His body jerks all night, the sheets are spotted with his blood.

It was 2 A.M.; the air was thick, like ink. He got in slowly, he was scared. I'd been sleeping, but I was scared now, too. I backed against the wall to make some space for him, then I was wedged between the wall and his cold form. Soon, I too, found breathing hard, but didn't speak; I wrapped him tightly in my arms instead—he'd just relaxed and was about to fall asleep. I tried to stay calm, but it was tight; I couldn't tell if I had merged with the wall, or with him. First, I felt invisible; then dead, entombed between a body and a wall. I tried to move, then finally said, "I'll hold you in our old bed, where there's room." He whispered that he liked it here, but I was firm. It was a matter of life or death.

I'm racing through the twilight now. The moon's white skin claims all the space above these fields. Beyond it, galaxies hang suspended, burning low. Shorebirds rise above pale shadows in the marsh. I'm flying now, into this strange light. There's alive and dead; happy, sad; light and darkness. That's all. On the radio, Black Uhuru's singing, *"What is life? Life is a spell."*

II

Form and Spirit

I'm driving through our past now. On the left is where we used to camp in summer. The run-down general store is on the rise above the beach. The old sign's still there, from twenty years ago, nailed to a pine: FILM ICE WORMS SODA FUN.

I'm hitting open country now. This is where he'd say, "Put on your lights," and I would argue, "No. I like the darkness, it's a challenge." I notice strange things here—you see more when you're alone: those oaks, spread wide; those fields, so green. It's dusk, his favorite time. Above the palms, a ghost moon waits in expectation of the night.

His last hospitalization, I walked right in. I've come to kiss your lips, I said, as I bent down. The man in the bed beside him slept, his mouth a cave that can't get air. COME BACK TO ME I called across the space. There must have been some sadness on my face because he waved me angrily away, his arm slicing the air, dragging its tubes behind. And so I turned and left the room. I could handle this because I'd already mourned him.

That night I curled up as though to die, but slept instead. It was a form of progress. Two words took shape inside my head: SPIRIT. FORM. I saw how we are consciousness, trapped inside these frames.

Everything begins with form. These fragile molds. See how

the spirit beats against them. It can't believe the lights will just go out.

The girl put it this way once in desperation: "He's dead, but he's still here. That messes up your mind." I know just what she means: when you embrace someone, you want them to be there.

I'm coming back to civilization: This land was nothing before it was this—just fields where crickets hummed at night. Now it's mostly malls, burning with an antiseptic kind of light—as though they'd sprung out of the innocent earth while you slept. I look in vain for landscape I could trust. Above the car, an egret wings over the freeway, tracking the lines of traffic, its slim weight poised, wobbling on currents of wind from racing cars; yet holding its course. It's strange, how we adapt: absence of pain now feels as happiness once did.

Dry leaves are blowing down the asphalt, bouncing over all six lanes, their sideways motion pulling my eyes away. Unbidden thoughts rise up with them, in the air beyond the windshield: *Imagine nonexistence.* This lane is going nowhere, so I switch. Leaves keep tumbling through the night. Sometimes, gripping the top of the wheel will make me feel alive.

This station's giving off trouble, so I change the dial. Now there's jazz: it moves along, inexorably as life. Fate lays down the beat; then you extemporize. I glance to the left lane, then to the right, seeking some connection; but the other drivers' eyes are straight ahead. The one in front slicks back his hair; he's looking in the rearview mirror—not at me, but at himself. His sticker is IMMORTALISTS DO IT FOREVER. Now I feel the freeway slip away, its dark surface washing sideways underneath my wheels. I am traveling at the speed of light. This is it, I think: I'm checking out. Leaving the road.

But I go back. You get up and start the day again because life is a habit, it's all you know. *I will* go on, I say. *I will* save him. *I will* survive. I looked up all the *I will* listings in the Phonolog, and it was strange—they all led back to you.

> *I Will* Always Love you
> Be There for You
> Be Your Friend
> Dance with You
> Drink the Wine
> Find a Way
> Follow You
> Get to You
> Love You Always
> Miss You When You Go
> Survive

The task seemed overwhelming: how could I be true to all those songs?

The bottles number sixteen now; sometimes they fall off the table, spilling the pills on the floor. He can't keep track. He's made a list, but can't interpret it. He holds it in his shaking hands and studies it. If you walk in on him then, he motions you away, stabbing the air with his good arm. "I'm trying to concentrate!" he'll scream when you try to help; then afterward bursts into tears.

I thought this would have an end, but it goes on.

I slide down beside him on the bed, the lines of our bodies echoing their past lives. "What's to become of us?" I whisper, but his ear is still.

He leaves the shower he has just begun to search for the shampoo. Beads of water roll down him to the floor. "It's where it always is," you say, but it's as though he doesn't hear. Or, hearing, doesn't comprehend. He sways like a flower on too long a stem, his legs spread in confusion, his fallen member a shadow between them. *Come back to me,* I sing, but all is silence. His eyes are coals, there's no reflection. As though they'd turned to stone from what they saw.

It's been raining for a week and all the leaves are down. I run faster now and take a new direction. I come upon a giant ginkgo tree—its leaves shed in a single moment: a blinding yellow circle wider than the boundaries of the tree. I throw myself on them, as though the light they cast could give back what I desire. I circle and run back through them again, their fallen brilliance drawing me. I sweep them in my arms; and then I see him standing there, our frail connection all in shadow now. I bury my face, remembering everything it once was to me; all it was to him, through me.

I'm going farther now, past the Canada geese, out past the lake. You see certain things with clarity out here: how, if you can bear to be alone, you lose the fear of being alone. How, if you are alone and are not loved, there is nothing left to lose— you're free. In prehistoric times, when climates froze, our ancestors moved on to stay alive. Flight was a form of adaptation then. Rounding the last curve in the trail, I think: He loved me to the best of his capacity, and beyond.

When I kiss his lips, I'm loving what they once expressed —their old life. I can't hold him anymore. I'm disappearing now.

Friends try to steady me, but I keep spinning. I write down the things they tell me so I'll know we've talked; so I'll know that I'm still here. They say things of comfort. They mean well, they are kind.

They are spirits who stand between me and some abyss. Their names come in the night. I say them in my mind—the way you'd speak of things your life depends on. They're like some cosmic hand within that reaches down to pull me from this dark.

Darkness, I think this: If he had died, he'd be at peace and we'd be free.

Now he is on Jupiter, and I'm on Mars. I call him through the gulf of space between us, but there is only silence now.

My boundaries break in many sites and drift to unseen places. I reach out quickly, invoking all the names. For what is your identity but the combined love of many, concentrated within.

"Get out of here!" he screams. "Can't you see I'm dying?"

We are fighting for our lives as insects do—clawing the air, their thin legs pedaling into nonexistence.

"We don't have a life!" the girl is crying now.

When he moves, his arms are out in front, extended into hostile space he cannot see.

A few friends never call again. Dying is an embarrassment: someone who failed.

People jumped from buildings once for less than this.

You imagine yourself as someone else—a character in a book. The pain no longer hurts, because it's hers. You describe her this way: *Tiring now, she wishes desperately to fall, to ride those tides out as far as they go.*

This life. It must be an experiment.

You strain like a hooked fish against this fate; then slowly weaken. Your silver scales dim.

• • •

I've abandoned you now, like a burned-out house: someone I could live in once. It happened when you screamed at me, your cold eyes seeing someone else, not me, your lips curled in avenues of lies. But when you paused for breath, I caught a glimpse—an old memory: the same lips slightly parted, sweet. The way they opened once for me.

You think you've built a thing for life; but what is life?

You try another posture; it might help: You double, folding into sorrow as though it offered light. Lean into it—as though the pain itself were consolation.

Darkness, tonight I swim in blackness, crying out. I call the friends, but all is silence. Pictures of them form, and then dissolve. But I keep at it, calling out. I imagine them, beside their names—a collective force that could keep me from some edge. But even as I call, I know there are no saviors. There is only the self, alone, in darkness—sometimes crying out, and sometimes silent.

I must rise above this, I say; but rising seems like taking leave of it forever.

The ways people leave the world: Sometimes you just go out, like a bulb.

When I hold myself at night, I can tell I'm still there; my flesh is warm.

Desire persists. Sometimes, you'll think: *Y* is the answer; and you see yourself with *Y*, in his arms. It is a kind of answer. Because in the end, you are alone. And after the end, you are nothing.

• • •

Darkness, I think this: The farthest I can go from here is death. But would it be enough?

This bridge I drive across so often; that kept you from me for so long: It dominates the landscape as it dominates my dreams and waking thoughts. I am forgetting the faces of those I love; it's impossible to remember what they had to offer once. I can no longer imagine the cosmic hand. All that comes to me is structure and suspension—an avenue between worlds.

I walk along its eastern side, my hand grazing the cool rail, wet with fog. I'm here now, it's a destiny. I pause and glance across the bay to where our life once was; then it just pulls me along: I have both legs over already. Looking down, I see the steely waters far below; I feel their unforgiving weight. I push off, it was easy. This is what birds know, except that gravity is swift—you don't have time to think. The impact was a shock; the water hard, like cement.

I enter the downward spiral now. I tried so hard to swim against the tide, but it keeps pulling me away from you, and from that shore we knew so long. It pulls me outward, toward the sea's imagined center. I still see the shore from time to time, through a mist of memory and old, forgotten feelings; and you there on it—pale, and small, and seeing me not ever anymore. I reach for you from habit, *I'm here, I'm here,* I call, searching for your eyes. But they're dead now, embers that have hardened and gone out. All is swept from sight: your figure and the shore; those arms that once belonged to me.

Our attachments—the ways they loosen. Those we have loved—the way their bodies, leaving, part the air around us in long tunnels of disbelief. Later, you can see the molecules re-forming, closing the space.

Now my arms falter, too, that struggled toward you for so long. They go under finally into darkness.

❧ LIFE ON EARTH ☙

I

ORMS COME, forms go; it's the story of life. How things
change shape, and slip away.

It's December now, the second year. When I say, "transplant," he chops his hand and waves the word away. "Don't talk
of that," he whispers. "I don't want to rock the boat." And then
I'll say, "The boat is sinking," because it's time he knew; the
doctors gave up long ago. In the beginning, there was nothing
wrong with him: his body shone, the way a horse's does in
certain light. He was golden when he loved. The horse was my
favorite animal, before him.

When I was young, my classmates used to play a game:
First, the leader said, "Choose a favorite COLOR." I'd write
down, "Red." Then she'd say, "Say three things about it. Its
qualities." And then I'd write: "It's warm. It's energetic. It's

strong." After COLOR would be ANIMAL. I always wrote down, "Horse. It's independent, yet a companion. It is spirited and proud. It's free." After ANIMAL came WATER. I used to think that strange: "Water's boring; there's nothing to be said," we'd all complain. When we were older, though, and played again, WATER was the center of attention. By then, I wrote: "My favorite body of water is a river. It's wild and active; it rushes on forever, it never ends." The last category was THE WHITE ROOM. "You are in a white room. It has no windows and no doors. Say three things about it." People hesitated here; the white room always stopped you. Some even left the game. I wrote: "I am in a white room. It has no entrance and no exit. The ceiling's white, as is the floor." I felt suffocated just imagining it. "It is nothing. It has no breath. It can't exist."

When the game was over, the leader interpreted responses: What you'd said about your color was supposed to represent the self—the way you saw it. The traits you gave the animal were what you'd look for in a friend. The qualities you gave your body of water reflected what you valued in your sexual life. The white room, of course, was death; I knew it from the start. No perceptions or sensation. What else could it have been?

He's almost gone; even the doctors are afraid. When I demand the conference now, they all agree as one. They don't consult their watches this time; they say out loud what must be done.

So now he's on the list. It's a hard thing to imagine someone on: a list to live. When I pass an accident, I no longer look away; I stare instead. *Are you the one?* Christmas is the time, the doctors say.

When he's not sleeping, he'll sometimes take a walk. He'll take four steps or so, then lean against a car. In the early months, I felt defiant: if people stared, I bore my eyes back into them, like knives, as though to cut out all the thoughts I knew were there. I was thinking them myself: the way he looked retarded—his face all twisted with the effort to stay erect. The way his thin frame shook, the trousers sliding down in back. When I'd try to straighten him, he'd push my hand away. I don't go with him anymore.

Yesterday, when I returned from work, the house was dark; but something unfamiliar on the table drew my eye: a glass vase filled with dark red roses, and next to it, a card. It struck me slowly: that it must be our anniversary. The children went together on the flowers. I sat down and stared at them intently, as if they'd come from him.

He was sleeping, somewhere in the house. The children helped him down the stairs and he sank quickly in his chair. His fingers curved above the arms, like claws. His body was hollow in the middle; his eyes stared straight ahead. A bottle of champagne and two small candles rose beside the flowers. The children worked the cork, then tipped the bottle into four thin glasses. I saw a box that wasn't there before; they whispered, *"It's from him." "Open it,"* she said, her eyes intense. *"I drove him to the antiques store where you get each other things for Christmas. He picked it out for you himself."*

"What's all the whispering about?" he whispered hoarsely, turning slow coal eyes on us.

The champagne stood untouched, its bubbles rising. I lifted mine and made the gesture of a toast. I gave him his, and we clicked lightly. He kept his in his lap, but I tipped mine back and drained it down. I didn't want to see the card. His writing was like hieroglyphics, and my eyes were clouding as I tried to read: *To my dearest, from a foreign land with love for you and thoughts only of the happiest things ahead for us.*

The box contained a shawl, all silk peach light; its fringes shimmered in the candlelight. It wrapped not once around, but doubled back again. It felt like being held and circled inside someone's arms.

"You're not going to cry again," he said, his voice still hoarse from medications.

I was wondering: will his flesh glow again someday, like this peach light?

"It's beautiful." I sank into his wintry arms.

"I want to take you somewhere special, when I'm better. I saw you wearing this." His voice came from somewhere far away—South America, perhaps, or Madagascar.

I whispered, "Were we dancing?"

I got up quickly, though. I couldn't let his fantasy take hold within my mind: the two of us arrested in that amber light, the music washing over us, the peach shawl wrapped around us as we glide slowly back to where we were before.

Late that night, I folded it. I slipped it back inside its still, white box.

If death is so natural, why are we afraid? I wonder: how far into darkness is it possible to go and still return? If I could accept this fate, would I find peace? I could ration strength that way, and then go on. But on to what? There are many, many endings; and most of them have happened. What is left, you wonder. Clouds? Weather? You're a detective now, on your way to some connection.

I can always drive away; the car's a last frontier. If you're patient, and your tank is full, eventually you'll come to country. By then, the stations start to fade; but you don't need the radio—you have weather, clouds, by then. This was on a half an hour ago, just before the road became two lanes:

> Oh baby, you so beautiful
> but you going to die someday.

Oh baby, I just want a little lovin'
before you pass away.

I see dark cattle fixed like statues in the shadow of a business park; a woman in a housedress, watering at sunset; pale apples spread in rings beneath the trees. The scenes pass by as swiftly as a life. This is not my world, I think, although the scenery is beautiful. The world I knew is gone. And this is not our life, but the life of someone in a movie: where they're trying to connect, but it doesn't work out, and the film ends. We weren't in this film.

The asphalt road is black, dividing fields of palomino grass. The muscled hills are half in shadow now. I'll be driving into darkness soon, the turquoise sky behind me with its rim of orange. But there's still light to see the signs: RIO ROAD RANCHETTES. CHAS. OTIS & SONS, PRIZE BULLS. Soon, I think, Chas. Otis will be dead; and then his sons will die, his sons' sons, too, and all his bulls. By then, there will be colonies in space.

He's weaker now. The holidays are over, even New Year's came and went. We didn't get a tree, but friends surprised us: they brought a tree and decorations, things to eat. We even danced, though we weren't happy; the needle would connect, and there would be a piece from back then, when we were. We drank a lot, and imitated past good times. Form's important. For instance, I'd come home from work and find my boy there, lying on the floor; he'd mourn for weeks in the same position. So I'd say softly: *Get up. You have to help me shop for food.* It was simple, in a way: you have to eat. When he isn't mourning, he rides. His bicycle responds to each command, and takes him far away from here.

Weekends are hard. I'll feel the loneliness beginning, then

lean into it, as one would a wind. I read the papers: one article referred to a Bereavement and Loss center, somewhere in New York. And I considered it: I could go to the Loss Center. But could it give him back to me?

Eventually, the questions all break through again—the kinds of things the children asked when small: "Why were we put here on this earth?" You had different answers for them then, back when things weren't filled with terror. Now you tell things to yourself, as though you were your child: you say, The choices are despair. And going on.

So you go on. But things keep popping up. Waiting does that. Sometimes, you suspend the thoughts of life on earth; but you still can't understand what happened. You'll be going along and suddenly remember it, and think: THAT THING—IT DIDN'T HAPPEN. It came flying toward us from Andromeda, faster than the speed of light. Your mind is always on it, even when you think it's somewhere else. It works day and night to answer all the questions—for instance: what to call it. It was a disaster, that is certain; but it wasn't a nuclear mishap. It was not a toxic event.

Another way to understand it: it is better than death; but not the same as life. This is not a life now, but an undiscovered state. You are learning as you go, tapping the cane in the dark. You wonder how it ends. You think: We'll be so tired by then, we'll just lie down. We'll have the strength to hold each other, nothing more. The only thing to pass between us is our history; it falls between the spaces where we breathe.

This is not LIFE as I dreamed it, but as it dreamed itself. You think of LIFE like this now: an experiment that failed. Yet sometimes, after rain, when the sky expands with light and rolling clouds move through it with the wind, you think that LIFE is like a great jazz riff. You sense the end the very moment you were wanting it to go on forever.

II

He lies there, strange and still, beneath new sheets. The surgeon wrapped it up at 9 P.M. We'd been here since early morning, in the solarium down the hall. It's a barren place—a station for people in extremity. The radiator in the corner hisses, then goes cold. The magazines are from last year. You want to leave, but can't; he might come out of surgery sooner than expected, and then you'd miss him. Or something might go wrong; and you could not forgive yourself if you were down the street in some neighborhood bar, or in the basement cafeteria. A bad coincidence would be with you all your life: say, if you were eating Fritos when he died; or knocking back a beer.

I know something will go wrong. I grip the metal armrests and stare ahead. My eyes avoid the children; their faces mirror everything that's in my heart, and I don't want to see that anymore. The friends who wait with us are better off; yet I imagine their relief, if this goes well, to finally be returning to their lives.

I was flipping through back pages when something caught my eye: an object wheeling down the hall beyond the open door. First, I saw a flash of white; and then his face above the sheet. He looked just like himself, asleep: flushed with life, his profile calm—as though he dreamed of rivers and horizons now, of things to come. We all jumped up and ran quickly after him. The surgeon trotted briskly by the gurney. He smiled and slowed his pace for us. "Everything went well," he said. (By the time the phone call finally came; by the time I heard the doctor's voice announce, "We have an organ now," I'd given up. "It's come," I said, the receiver sticking to my hand. By then, he thought I meant United Parcel. "What's come?" he said, not even looking up.)

If you dwelled on implications, you'd be torn in two. But they come to you unbidden: that someone had to die so he could live. That someone grieves as you once did, still do; but theirs is fresh, and yours seems ancient, thin and stale. That you are lucky—*in a way*: for they will only have to do it once, but yours will come again.

The organ beats within him now, exploring its new home. Already, he's half sitting in the bed; he smiles. "Who won the game?" he whispers clearly, in his own voice. We laugh quickly, in relief. These can't be his first words—you expected revelation: How it feels, returning from the dead. In the other bed, his roommate also waits to hear the score. He has the other kidney; they are brothers now. TRANSPLANT FEVER was the headline that week.

I try imagining the donor: male or female, rich or poor, reckless or contemplative, miserable or kind; and what the end was like. It's better they don't tell you; because eventually, you must turn to other things. You continue on. But there is something in the mystery, the endless possibilities, that keeps you thinking. Did he wear a leather jacket on the night he met his fate? Did her foot slip on the pedal when she meant to stop? I look around the ward, at all the faces: they're dead, and yet they live again. The spreads across their sheets are white. The walls are white, the tiles beneath them, too. Their gowns, the sinks. Is this THE WHITE ROOM? The one I feared so long?

The weeks slide by. Nurses post his figures with the others in the hall. Substances go into him by day and mingle with the organ there in strange cooperation. His facy is rosy now, like Reagan's—flushed with life. This place appears to be a building on a hill, where day and night swift elevators glide from earth to sky. But in reality, it is a city of the future: where people who were born before lie wrapped in newborn expectation.

While he waits, I wait for him. It's January now, and cold. On the beach a few old men are casting in the surf, but otherwise the sand is empty—unbroken as a desert. I stand here on the edge and think of form. And I consider mine—the way he loved it once. He watches his new body day and night; observes it coming back.

I think how this reverses everything. The way it makes an ending not an end.

The morning paper carries news of odd discoveries: at the bottom of the ocean, strange new forms of life. A creature with six sides and rows of hard black dots was found in fossil rock they date at sixty million years or more. Then there were the pale blind shrimp: feeding on invisible bacteria from underwater geysers whose locus is the center of the earth.

III

When they release him, when they finally let him go, I travel north. I resume my work; and he goes back to his. They watch him, though; he checks in every week. He takes his first steps back.

I go as far away as the continent allows. It is winter here: fields of snow, all purity and light. It's nothing like the beach back there—those little wisps of wind, the chill before the fog wears off. Here, things that can't find shelter freeze at night. You see their tiny shapes stiffening in the morning light. Here, all is endless fields of white. Forgetting to remember him becomes a kind of bliss. In the night, though, I know who I am; the same moon follows me, remembering everything that went before.

Some days, I go out on skis across the snow, as far as breath can reach—those points on the horizon that mark the limits of what the eye can see, or know. And I go into darkness: the woods at night. It is a new dimension, no worse than any other. All things there are strange; yet no stranger than before. When the moon is high, all light is blue: the grounded snow below; the ravenous fields of stars above. All things hang suspended in that silent chill. Indoors, they speak of things like acid rain. But I can hear the night owl call; see tracks that move as shadows on the fields of ice.

In my dream, Peggy Lee sang "Fever," and all was as it was before.

In the meantime, astronomers are trying to understand the dark of night. The papers ask: Why is the night sky dark?

If all goes well, he'll join me here. We'll look each other over, wondering, Who are you? We will circle, as animals do, and watch for signs.

When I left, he said, "I've come to see things through your eyes." He meant the world, which by then meant realities he could no longer see: simple things, like leaves. "I never noticed certain things until you gave voice to them," he said. So this is how I see myself now: his seeing-eye person.

I left in early morning, before the sun was up, and saw for both of us: The full moon going down across the bay—huge, and shadowed like a stone. And later, at the airport, the flame of sun, its crown—liquefied between the eastern hills. They hung suspended there in balance, on the rims of opposite horizons.

Here, the air flashes in your lungs like lightning. Stands of birch are cased in ice—their narrow branches coated, and clicking in the wind. I've finally reached the ridge; it's early, song birds cry in frozen air. I think of him. *Imagine trees of glass,* I say. *White meadows. Moons like paper, pale and white.*

Suspend your fear, I tell myself, or else the end is always with you.

Now he's coming back to me. He's here. It seems that everything is as it was before. He walks erect, his eyes are filled with light. I think: We never asked for life; and yet, once in it, we accept. Could we have imagined it, before we knew? Were we forms back then, or just ideas for the future? But I say nothing. He is back. The moon is large with newly risen light. We walk together through the snow, past yellow lights in houses on a hill. The houses make me think how, in the other life, we were always finding ways to be secure. Yet here, the animals of the field—see the way their eyes dart, their noses sense the wind. Always looking behind, and to the side. Tomorrow, he will know the ridge: the fields of whiteness, their filaments of light. The meadow where the sun stings birch trees into song. *There is white,* I'll say, *that is not death.*

In the night, a fire burns low—the first on earth: a core of light within a darkened room. We are alone at last, high above the fields of snow. My arms reach up and slide around the form. We're blind now, feeling for lost connections in dark seas.

IV

The doctors warned of this. They used the phrase, "rejection episode"—nothing plain, like "failure." I liked "episode" the best of anything they said: something happens briefly, then is gone. Later, you say, "Oh, that. That little episode." Patients often have one in the first six months; sixty percent, they say. He's gone over five now; everything's okay, you tell yourself. Everything's okay with us.

You know rejection, though; you'd recognize it anywhere. He's going down again. But we saw the fields of light, you want to say.

You're hearing voices now. You listen—it's their turn. What do they say? the doctor wants to know. He hasn't heard of hearing voices since his intern days. The early texts. They aren't instructing me to kill, you reassure. You guide him through this. It's more like static, radio noise—the sound of voices when you flip the dial around. Once you've got that clear, they slow their pace; the more you speak, the fewer voices crowd your head at night. They're still competing, though, fighting one another for air time. Those sounds within—the things you can't say:

You love him, leave him, abandon him, forget him, will it last? What last? Oh, the organ, the thing, the mystery. It's a matter of chemistry, fate, luck, chance, time. But what if what if what if. And then, whichever way, what should you do, say? How should you behave, think? Should you look ahead, look behind, or stick to the present? In what ways are you there? Not there? In what ways do you withdraw, love, hate, avoid, wish, regret, deny? And then there's the future: will you fear it forever now? Or just in different ways? It could happen any time time time. Or. It could go on and on and on. Why, really, when all is said and done: You could be hit by a truck, just crossing the street. That would be a quirk of a twist of. And he'd go on, afterward. And that would be it. More or less. Less or more. You just don't know. That's the thing. Now? Or later? This is just AN AMPLIFICATION. Of what we all. Come to. In the end.

In the meantime, there are all these rocks in the road. Fault lines, rifts. Land mines from World War II.

The doctor nods. Or grimaces, or smiles. Both, or all, and always sympathetically. This is not his problem. But he feels it when you speak. It's just this: It's your problem, not his. You are in this alone. Everyone else is in theirs alone, too. You'll never understand it—there are so many of us, billions; yet everyone's alone.

So, how is your (organ mind heart health spirit)? you ask, when you can finally speak. Me? he says? I'm just fine. Just fine just fine just fine.

You do ask it. It is inevitable. You ask yourself: Are you crazy?

Seven weeks pass by. They come, then go. He checks in with the doctors at the clinic. They go over him. He's their man in space. The elevators in the building still go UP and DOWN. The arrows still point Red and Green.

When you drive in to pick him up, you have to pull in the NO WAITING zone, and they sometimes move you on.

Then you go around the block.

You pull up again, but he's still inside.

You turn the volume up.

The fourth pass, you'll sometimes go for cappuccino. What the hell. Fuck him. Fuck them. Fuck it.

The fifth pass, he's on the curb. You can tell he's fuming. "Where the hell were YOU?" he'll finally say.

Every now and then, you recall your previous life. Or visions of the life to come.

This was the week they predicted the massive extinctions: a million species could die by 2000, the scientists said. Was there life on other planets? you wondered then. And would theirs last?

• • •

The chemistries go down down down. He comes back. Goes on. As before. Things are finally getting better. Or so they say. He's going on. But you're still rooted to the spot. You mourned him once, and let him go. When he came back, you thought: we go on from here. But now he's coming back a second time. You could reconnect with him; but he could leave again. He could check out any time.

This is different from anything you've ever known. When the voices come at night, you say, Get out, I've got this UNDER CONTROL. But your heart's still beating double time; it could audition for the band.

They've increased the drugs. His voice is high again, his speech is fast—45 rpm, like Donald Duck.

The boy is on his bicycle. He points the wheel toward the road's imagined center, and rides. Our girl is back in school. "I've been trying to phone," I'll say. "Were you in the studio all night?" She's an artist, now. She creates and enters other worlds. "No," she says. "I've been working in the morgue."

I am silent. I think of Leonardo, the lessons of anatomy. "I was trying to stretch the limits of my perception," she explains.

I was their center once. They came into me; then out.

I see the headline in the morning: REACTOR CORE IS BURNING INTO EARTH.

It's only natural to wonder: could there be things still worse than this? Perhaps an intergalactic event. Something that would blow the planet off its axis and send us spinning, breathless, in the void.

That night, I dream of deer in Colorado: the way they step down to the river in winter, thrusting their lips into its slowly moving light. The way the river hardens in the cold, its power stopped—as though freezing had transformed it into alien, static form. An icy suspension, standing for what's gone.

V

We settle slowly into this new life. Certain knowledge, permanent and strange, is with us now—a shadow hovering beside our forms, moving left as we move left. As if we'd caught a glimpse of the invisible, and it moved swiftly into us.

Yesterday, a man brought suit against the government. He was in the army in the fifties, back when it was tested—the first atomic bomb survivor, in his way. He described it: a light so bright that when he closed his eyes and covered them, he saw his bones. He carries it inside him now, an indelible impression: the form within.

Climates change, unlocking the past to live again and repeat itself. How are we to meet this thing? I ask. Rise as rivers rise, their ice crusts cracking on the thaw?

His hands will ride along my limbs. "Your leg is straight and thin," he'll say. "A tree." A part of me that was always special to his hand. "You're growing hard," I'll say. "A rock." And he may whisper, "Yes, I am a rock." His lips are soft, like organisms blinking slowly in warm tides. I feel the pull of earth against my back, its center hot. Anything is possible there.

Some say there's more, beyond this life. That we will rise, at last, above all grief.

We could be weightless, soaring far beyond the planet we have loved.

But it is spinning underneath us now, drawing us toward the fire within. We are here. This is our time, our life on earth.

ABOUT THE AUTHOR

Sheila Ballantyne was born in Seattle, Washington. She is the author of two novels, *Norma Jean the Termite Queen* and *Imaginary Crimes*. She lives in Berkeley, California, and teaches at Mills College.